"I don't ██████████████████ **o right to ki** ████

He wondered ██████████████ 'd kissed her or that he'd stopped. From the way her chest was hitching with every breath, his money was on the latter. Still, she was fighting the attraction.

"That was not a kiss."

"Excuse me? I know when I've been kissed," she said breathily.

"*This* is a kiss." Mason reached for her, molding his hands on either side of her face, and pressed his lips to hers....

Jenna Bayley-Burke is a domestic engineer, freelance writer, award-winning recipe developer, romantic novelist, cookbook author and freebie fanatic. Blame it on television, a high-sugar diet, or ADHD; she finds life too interesting to commit to one thing. Except her high-school sweetheart and two blueberry-eyed baby boys. She hides out in the Pacific Northwest, where it doesn't rain half as much as people think.

JUST ONE SPARK...

BY
JENNA BAYLEY-BURKE

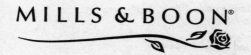

MILLS & BOON®

All the characters in this book have no existence outside the imagination of the author, and have no relation whatsoever to anyone bearing the same name or names. They are not even distantly inspired by any individual known or unknown to the author, and all the incidents are pure invention.

First published in Great Britain 2006
Harlequin Mills & Boon Limited,
Eton House, 18-24 Paradise Road, Richmond, Surrey TW9 1SR

© Jenna Bayley-Burke 2006

ISBN 0 263 84988 0

Set in Times Roman 10½ on 12 pt.
171-0506-60342

Printed and bound in Spain
by Litografia Rosés S.A., Barcelona

CHAPTER ONE

SCANNING the line for the third time, Hannah crossed her legs tighter and tried to concentrate. But to no avail. The sensual scene unfolding on the pages proved no match for the sound of pocket change tumbling around in the dryer. With a reluctant sigh she set down her book, cover side down, chanting the page number. No one in the laundromat needed to know she read steamy romance novels.

She jumped off the washing machine and went to the wall of dryers to listen for the clanking of the loose change, leaning close to the machine spinning her jeans to be sure. She opened the door with a tug and reached in, removing the mood-breaking quarter. With a yelp she tossed the hot metal in the air. Shaking her singed hand, she watched as the coin rolled across the floor, right to the pay phone. Well, wasn't that just ironic?

Ignoring her lost change, Hannah hopped back atop the washing machine. She found her place in the book and carefully folded the cover over so no one saw the shirtless man leaning over the woman barely covered by a sheet.

Hannah grinned as the washer below her kicked into the spin cycle. She'd timed it perfectly. Her sweaters would be ready to take home and lay out at the same time the rest of her laundry finished drying. The efficiency of her weekly washing routine thrilled her almost as much as what was transpiring on the pages she eagerly returned to.

The roguish hero, a modern-day pirate, finally kissed the heroine. Hannah's eyes scanned the pages, rushing the duo to the good parts. His finger was tweaking a rosebud nipple as Hannah began to feel herself warm to the ministrations of the washing machine.

"Lose something?" a gravelly voice said, far too close for comfort.

Flustered, Hannah closed her book. "Excuse me?" she asked, keeping her head down and praying the heat rising from her shoulders did not look like a blush. She didn't want to be caught doing anything blush-worthy in the neighborhood laundromat.

"I think this is yours." She noticed the gold band on his left hand and decided not to bother with his face.

"Oh, thank you," she replied, taking the quarter and plunking it beside her.

"Maybe it's a sign," he said.

Hannah reminded herself to be nice, neighborly even. Maybe he was just making conversation.

"A sign?" she asked, looking up.

Wow. No wonder he was married. The man was designed specifically with breeding in mind. From the spiky tips of his warm brown hair to the ends of his steel-toed black boots he was yummy. The tight T-shirt with the fire-department logo did nothing to hide his muscled chest. She even allowed herself to gaze down his navy work pants and check out the fit. Fantastic.

"The quarter rolled right to the pay phone. Maybe there's someone who wants you to call." The single dimple on his left cheek made his cocksure grin all the more devilish.

Hannah smiled. "I don't think so." She turned to her book and pretended she hadn't just replaced the cover hero with this fireman in her fantasy.

"You sure? Your boyfriend maybe?" he asked.

Here we go again. "No boyfriend, and it takes more than a quarter to make a phone call these days," she said without looking up.

"Lucky for me." Confidence dripped from his words. Sickening. Not even worth playing with in her fantasies now. What a shame. Back to the cover model, even if he was probably gay.

She ignored the jerk as he cocked a hip on the washer, close to her knee.

"Hey, this thing is on." He placed his hand on the top, much too close to her hip.

She wasn't about to let him pass judgment on her for adding spice to her reading by selecting an inspiring location. Or broadcast the fact to the entire establishment. "I'm sure you have things to do," she shot at him without looking up.

"Actually, I was thinking after you were done here we could do something together. A drink, or a cup of coffee?"

"Really?" She looked up at his face. His eyes were a beautiful middle-of-the-ocean blue. Too bad he was such an ass. "I don't think so."

"If you already have plans tonight I'm off tomorrow," he said, moving his hand closer until it brushed her thigh.

"You're off all right." The three dryers opposite her powered off one by one. As if on cue, the washer beneath her ran down.

"Hmm?" he asked, watching as she gathered up her clothes.

Not bothering to fold, she stuffed the laundry into pillowcases and turned to go. "I don't date married men."

"What?" A look of horror flashed across his face.

"Next time, you might want to take the ring off first," she spat at him, pointing to his hand.

"Oh, man. I forgot that was there." He tried to say something more but the words flew behind her as she marched out of the building.

From the landing of her building next door, she noticed he'd actually followed her outside. She quickly ducked up another flight of stairs. At the next landing she peered out. He was still on the sidewalk outside, standing there playing with the ring on his finger.

Forgot it was there. As if.

"Your experiment was a total bust." Mason flung the gold ring across the booth at his brother. "I don't know what I was thinking. Thanks to you, the hottest woman I've ever seen thinks I'm a total sleaze."

"Really?" Derek immediately opened his notebook. "Tell me your observations."

"I'm not one of your experiments. If I hadn't been coming off a twenty-four-hour shift I never would've let you put that thing on my hand."

"Interesting hostility." Derek scribbled a few notes. "Tell me more," he said as a pretty blonde waitress set down a pitcher of beer and two mugs.

"I guessed you'd want the usual, Mason?" she said, batting her eyelashes.

"Thanks, Tanya." He gifted her with a grin as she slinked away.

"She likes you." Derek stated the obvious. "Have you two, you know?"

"No!" Mason shook his head in offense. "Tanya can't carry on a conversation that's not about sex."

"You say that like it's a bad thing."

"Have at it, Derek." Mason poured the beer into a frosty mug. "I prefer someone who can talk about anything and everything."

"Yet you were just talking about the hottest woman you'd ever seen. Were you interested in her physically or intellectually? Tell me more about that." Derek pushed his wire-rimmed glasses up his Roman nose.

"You're creeping me out with your psychologist talk. Knock it off." Mason took a long, slow drink. Derek had a point, but he didn't have to know that. "I just came to give you your ring back and tell you your hypothesis sucked. Women do not come on to married men more than unmarried ones."

"It's a working theory. I have to tweak it a bit before I present it at the university." Derek stared down at his notes. "Exactly how many women came on to you?"

"Four," Mason admitted. He'd already gone through with the experiment as his brother had asked—might as well tell him what had happened. "Two at the grocery store, a waitress and a florist."

"Tanya doesn't count. You had the ring off and she seems to know you."

"I wasn't counting her." Mason smiled. "I made sure they all plainly saw the ring, just like you said. The florist actually gave me her number on the back of a card."

"*Tell me* that's unusual for you."

Mason shrugged. "Not really."

Derek rolled his eyes. "Why were you at a florist anyway? Trying to impress a lady?"

Mason leaned forward, narrowing his eyes. "*Tell me* you didn't forget Mom's birthday."

Derek's eyes widened. "Damn. You didn't remind me. Is it today or tomorrow?"

Mason shook his head. "You so owe me. For doing this stupid experiment and putting your name on the card. When I find this woman, you will make her understand that you're the one who put me up to wearing that ring."

"Whatever," Derek said, not looking up from his notebook. "Why bother if she thinks you're some adulterous loser?"

"You didn't see her. She was absolutely stunning. Silky brown hair and creamy skin with freckles. And her eyes were two different colors. They were both kind of hazy gray, but one was blue and the other was green."

Derek's head popped up. "You're not supposed to be attracted to that. It's asymmetrical. Symmetry is what's attractive."

Mason shrugged. "I thought it was hot."

Derek shook his head. "It must be her waist-to-hip ratio. That's another thing that attracts men."

Mason sighed. Her waist-to-hip ratio was pretty spectacular. But those eyes had made him cross the room. The fact that she had been reading a trashy romance novel while sitting on a washer during the spin cycle had kept her in his thoughts ever since.

"Another pig?" Kate asked, gulping down her apple martini.

From their perch at the corner table, the three women had a perfect view of the happenings at the martini bar. Just right for people-watching, or, more typically, laughing at the latest disasters in their love lives.

"I'm telling you, it's like they have radar or something." Hannah ran her finger around the rim of her wineglass. "They must see me and think 'Hit on her, she'll never guess.'" She waved her hand through the smoky air of the lounge. "Please."

"At least someone is hitting on you." Molly chimed in, all sunshine and light. "That has to be flattering, right?"

"Leave it to you to look on the bright side, sweetie." Kate turned in her seat to catch the bartender's attention and signaled for another round of drinks. "Before happy hour is over," she explained to her friends.

"They're all cheats, pigs, or dogs. The whole lot of them." Hannah watched the lights reflect in her white wine as she swirled the glass.

"Not all of them," Molly said sweetly. She'd married her high-school sweetheart, Troy, the week after college graduation. Hannah liked to think Troy's continued fidelity had something to do with the drunken threat she made the eve of his wedding to castrate him if he ever dared cheat on her sister. But she knew it probably had a lot more to do with her sister's extensive lingerie collection.

"Troy is an anomaly," Hannah replied as a waitress delivered the second round of drinks. She eyed her sister's cranberry juice with a twist of lime, hoping Molly was just tired as she claimed. It was bad enough her baby sister had been married for five years. Molly couldn't possibly have a baby before she did too. Hannah closed her eyes against the ugly thought. It was just turning thirty that was making her think of babies.

She had more than a full month until she was officially out of her twenties. And she wouldn't be twenty again for all the shoes in Nordstrom's. No, she liked being wiser, she just didn't like feeling that somewhere along the line she'd missed a step and fallen behind.

"Did I tell you I have to spend six weeks in Klamath Falls?" Kate asked, sipping at the bright green liquid in her glass. "They moved up the trial date for my toxic mold case. I'm heading down on Monday to do some prep work. I'll be there clear through the holidays. You'll have the place all to yourself," she said to her roommate.

"Ugh. The armpit of Oregon. Won't you be coming home on weekends?" Hannah asked.

"No way!" Kate said, taking a long draw of her martini. "I get a plane ticket every weekend. Why waste it coming back to Stumptown? I have to be here the rest of the year."

Hannah shrugged and sipped at her drink. The freedom would be nice if she needed it, but she liked bumping into Kate in the bathroom. It was nice to talk to someone on a daily basis who didn't speak in retail acronyms.

Her sister's hand was warm on her arm. "Come over next week. I'll have a party. You can meet some nice people."

Kate laughed and swallowed the last of her drink. "I'm glad I'll be out of town. Your fixer-upper parties are a mess."

Hannah giggled as her sister and friend squabbled over the merits of matchmaking. It was like being in a cartoon and watching the angel and devil battle it out on her shoulders. Yin and yang. She always had to sit between them or Kate might come out swinging, though Molly's quiet barbs were far more lethal.

Hannah stopped smiling as she considered what her sister had just said. Party to Molly meant a chance to play matchmaker. Without Kate there to laugh at their prospects she'd be forced to play nice. The horror.

Hannah rolled over and flipped on the lamp. Just like every night for the last week, sleep eluded her. The numbers on her alarm clock mocked her, a digital reminder she had to be at work at five a.m. to get the markdown team rolling through the store.

She didn't mind getting in early. It gave her a chance to move fixtures around without having to worry about customers tripping over them. Since she hadn't been able to sleep all week, getting up any earlier than she had to was a chore.

Pulling open the drawer of her nightstand, she took out one of her romance novels. She had to think of something else, someone else. The image that kept creeping into her mind sickened her. She needed to fill her head with another man, a noble man to make her forget all about him.

Opening the pages, she began to read. The little paperbacks shipped to her mailbox each month were Hannah's vacation. She used them to travel without leaving the room, to relax without having to finagle time off. Her tired eyes scanned the well-read passages, flipping ahead to the good parts.

Hannah thought herself a sensual, sexual person so much so, it had bothered her first steady boyfriend. She would be, if she gave herself half a chance. But ever since she'd found out Marty, a man she'd dated for almost a year, had actually been married with three young children, she no longer trusted her instincts where men were concerned.

She'd been so stupid. Never questioning why she only had a work and cell number for him, never thinking it odd that she met so few of his friends. It wasn't until Molly and her husband Troy had double-teamed her that she realized the truth. Troy had hired a private investigator, providing her with pictures of Marty's wife and babies.

She still hadn't believed it, and when she'd confronted him he'd flown off the handle, had said she was being controlling, high maintenance. Then he'd made some lame excuse about having another phone call and she'd never heard from him again.

Worse than anything had been the humiliation. Her friends and family had all suspected, had all been scheming the best way to approach her. It sickened her to think how they'd whispered behind her back. Thankfully, no one from work knew. It would be hard to convince upper management she could run a multimillion-dollar department store when she made such a disaster out of her personal life.

Still, she was a healthy woman with certain needs. That was where the books came in handy. Each month she found four new men in her mailbox. Four heroes to romance her and fuel her fantasies. It had worked pretty well, up until her little run-in with the married fireman last week.

At least she thought he was a fireman. Maybe it had just been some T-shirt his wife had laid out for him that morning.

His wife was the reason she was having trouble staying asleep. Every time she let herself dream, she wound up horizontal with him. It always woke her up with a jolt. She'd unknowingly been the other woman once. She'd never do it again.

Letting out a resigned sigh, Hannah rolled to her side, and drank in the scene between the heroine and the man she thought was a gigolo. She followed them upstairs to the hotel room, heat pooling in her belly as the would-be gigolo began to strip off the heroine's clothes piece by piece until she was left in nothing but stockings and garter belt.

Hannah pressed the body pillow between her legs as he kissed his way down the heroine's body. Squeezing her thighs together, she read how he licked her right there, how the heat from him conflicted with the feel of her buttocks pressed against the cool glass of the hotel-room window. Hannah held the book open with one hand. Anyone might be watching them, becoming as aroused as she was.

As the heroine's knees buckled and they moved to the bed Hannah laid the book down. She closed her eyes and imagined it was her he touched, her hands mimicking his mouth.

She visualized him between her legs, felt the crisp tips of his hair as she massaged his scalp. She moaned as her muscles began to clench and spasm. She matched the rhythm, making the orgasm last as long as possible. She felt him move up her body, leaving hot little kisses in his wake. Stubble scratched against her nipples. Reaching for him, she opened her eyes.

Her heart stopped. It was *him*. The blue-eyed adulterer was in her bed, smiling up at her.

Hannah found herself panting, sitting straight up in her bed, the blankets tangled at her feet. Her fists were clenched as she worked to catch her breath.

"Not again," she groaned, flopping back against the pillows. "Never again."

"They said what?" Derek asked, chuckling under his breath.

Mason kicked him hard under the table. He did not deserve to be laughed at. "If it weren't for you and your stupid hypothesis, I wouldn't have spent every spare moment in that damned coffee shop anyway."

He'd become infatuated with finding her, the woman with two different-colored eyes. He'd even found the book she was reading, a paperback steamier than anything he'd ever read in *Penthouse*. It had him dreaming of doing every single trick in the book to her. A woman that beautiful, brazen enough to read erotica while sitting on a spinning washing machine in public—it made his jeans dig into his crotch.

"She might have just not been into you, you know," Derek shot back.

He'd thought of that a lot over the last few days. Even if he found her and was able to make her understand he wasn't a total jerk, he still might have blown it with her. Mason shook his head hard to dispel the thought. He still had to try.

He wasn't obsessed because she'd turned him down. It came from the way he'd felt standing next to her. Electric, aroused, alive with possibility. He had to find her, if only to find out he'd imagined it.

"Too bad most of my charm lives in your imagination." He slumped back against the leather booth.

"That's it, lash out at me. Your anger has to go somewhere." Derek grinned.

"You think this is funny? I had to explain to three different people that I'm not a stalker. They still might call the police. I know every cop in that precinct. I'll be a laughingstock!"

After finishing a twenty-four-hour shift, Mason had spent the morning in the coffee house. Not too unusual, except he'd stayed there for four hours, just as he had for the last three days. Today an employee had asked what he was doing. He'd explained, hoping for help in finding his mystery lady. But she hadn't thought his interest was romantic. She'd thought he was a stalker.

"If you think about it, you are a little obsessed. Maybe you are stalking this woman. Maybe they have a right to be concerned about the guy commandeering a window seat and ogling women as they enter the building next door. Just look at it objectively."

"I don't want to hurt her, Derek. I just want a chance to explain." He knew it sounded strange, but he had to see her again. It wasn't some psychological imbalance; it was a physical need.

"How long has it been?" Derek poured the last of the beer into his empty mug.

"What are you talking about?" Mason took a long swallow from his own mug.

Leaning closer, Derek whispered, "Since you've had sex?"

Mason nearly choked. "None of your damned business." *Too long.* "You're the one who's consumed by sex, not me."

Unless it is sex with her. He didn't care to listen to sociological reasoning or psychobabble right now.

Derek ignored the jab. "Maybe you're just fixating on this woman because you need a sexual release."

Mason clenched his jaw. She had starred in every one of his dreams since they had met. But his need to make things right with her was more about the way he felt when he'd seen her. As if he was magnetically drawn to her.

"That's not it. There is something about her. I don't expect you to understand; I just expect you to help me explain why I was wearing a ring."

Derek shook his head. "Just don't get arrested. You may have an explanation for the ring, but you don't have any excuse for stalking the woman."

CHAPTER TWO

"THERE'S a biological basis for men having more spouses than women. Women have control over whom they will mate with. They have to be choosy because they can only have a limited number of offspring and so make fewer pairings," Derek addressed the party.

What an idiot. "Men just can't keep it in their pants," Hannah said from her perch on a barstool in Molly's kitchen. This was Molly's bachelor number one? "Their wives keep divorcing them and they keep remarrying so they never have to learn how to pick up their own dirty socks. *That's* why men marry more than women."

He pushed his glasses further up his narrow nose. "Historically women are the ones more likely to cheat, especially around ovulation. They seek out the alpha male to mate with, but the beta male to live with. It's women who have their cake and eat it too, not the other way around."

"You have got to be kidding me!" Hannah plunked her beer down on the counter with a thud.

"He knows his stuff." Bachelor number two tried to defend Derek. "He has a Ph.D."

"I don't care what his degree is; his theory doesn't hold water," Hannah said, her eyes narrowed and ready for battle.

"To be fair, Hannah, neither does yours." Troy moved between the two warring factions. "You can't reduce people to generalizations."

Hannah pursed her lips together and squinted at her brother-in-law. For a brief moment she thought about telling him exactly what he and his friends could do with their theories. But then half the room erupted into hoots and hollers when one team scored a touchdown.

Hannah retreated upstairs to finish her laundry. Slamming the dryer door shut, she flipped the machines on and checked her watch. Her laundry would be done at about the same time as the game ended. Which was what she'd planned, but now she wished she could just bail.

Closing the laundry room door behind her, she went slowly down the stairs. At the bottom she turned to go into the kitchen and paused. Troy and Molly stood all wrapped up in each other; their heads bowed sharing secrets.

Spinning back around, Hannah went up a few steps and sat on the stairs. It wasn't right to be jealous of her sister. She hugged her knees to her chest and allowed herself an indulgent moment of heartache. Why hadn't she found a man who looked at her that way?

Troy wasn't perfect—he was too tall, bossy and completely sports obsessed—but his quirks never bothered Molly. Why couldn't she find a man whose oddities didn't drive her crazy? Hannah realized everybody had their faults, but she had a knack for finding the guys who needed professional help. The last guy she'd gone on a date with had major credit problems, and the one before him had talked to his mother on his cell phone during dinner—twice.

Tonight's pool of suitors wasn't any more promising. One laughed like a cartoon character, another had reached thirty without leaving the nest, and there was Professor Know-It-

All and his ridiculous notions. No one even remotely interesting, and yet she'd promised Molly she would go out with one of them. She just couldn't win.

Hannah wished she were attracted to just one of them. Adrenaline coursed through her as she thought of the way she'd reacted to the cheating pig at the laundromat. Sure, he was good-looking, but something about him stuck in her brain. And her dreams. Why couldn't she just feel like that about one of these guys?

"Sorry, I didn't know anyone was up here."

Hannah jumped at the sound. Professor Know-It-All in the flesh. She scooted to the side of the staircase. "Take a left at the top of the stairs. The bathroom is the first door on the right."

"Thanks," Derek said, placing a foot on a riser. With his hand on the railing, he paused and looked down at Hannah. "I'm sorry if I upset you before. Sometimes I forget I'm talking to friends and not students. My brother tells me not to give my opinion to people who aren't specifically paying to hear it, but I don't listen to him as often as I should."

Hannah smiled in acknowledgement. A wordy apology was better than none. "It's not you; it's a touchy subject for me."

"Oh," Derek said. His mouth formed the vowel far longer than the word hung in the air. "Adultery is interesting to me." He sat down below her on the stairs, looking up at her, and continued. "I've always found it fascinating. I've worked on all sorts of studies about what causes people to cheat. I'm working out a theory that married men may wander because women hit on them more."

"What?" Hannah asked, feeling her temperature drop.

"I was thinking women proposition married men more. It makes sense. Women would know going in the man is a provider and women who only want sex wouldn't have to deal with the emotional side."

"You're insane," Hannah spat. Was that why she hadn't seen the red flags in her relationship with Marty? "When a woman gets involved with a married man it's because she doesn't know he's married. And he doesn't tell her."

Derek shrugged and looked up at her. "You might be right, but you might be wrong. I'm looking to find out."

"Don't waste your time. If women see a ring they look the other way." Hannah examined Derek's face as he spoke. There was something vaguely familiar about him. She must have seen him at one of Troy and Molly's parties before.

"Not all women." Derek shifted on the step and his eyes widened. "Hey, your eyes are two different colors."

Ignoring his comment, Hannah continued. "Men don't cheat because some woman comes on to them. They cheat because they're pigs and can't keep it zipped. Cheaters get off on fooling women into thinking they care. They do it for the thrill, not because a pretty girl makes it easy."

"Did you…were you…?" Derek stammered. Finally, Mr Opinions didn't have one. Hannah hoped he wasn't trying to ask exactly why the subject was touchy for her. He cleared his throat. "So you have never propositioned a married man?"

"Never would." Marty had romanced her for months before she'd slept with him. She never would have even had a drink with him had she known he was married.

"And if a man came on to you that you suspected was married?" Derek asked, leaning back. Hannah noticed he stared directly into her eyes instead of looking her up and down the way most men did.

"If he had his ring on I wouldn't let it get that far. Most guys take it off. You can't tell they're married if their pocket is full of gold."

Derek shook his head vigorously and swallowed hard. "Do married men hit on you?"

Hannah laughed. "I'm something of an anomaly. It seems like every man who hits on me is married. Just last week some guy tried to pick me up at the laundromat. It was disgusting. His wife's clothes were probably in the washing machine. The pig didn't even bother to take off his ring. And his excuse was stellar. He said he forgot it was on. Can you imagine?"

Hannah shook her head, and reminded herself she hated the pig, no matter how sexy he was.

Derek appeared to be laughing at her misery. It would be funny if it had happened to someone else. If she hadn't dreamt of the man every night since.

Clearing his throat, Derek said, "I'd like to talk more about your theories. Maybe we could meet for coffee. Do you live out this way?"

Coffee? She hated coffee. "I live downtown, not far from the university campus actually. I'm swamped with work, though."

"My schedule is pretty flexible," he said with a smile.

One meeting might get Molly off her back.

"Tuesday morning? I don't have to be in to work until the afternoon." Hannah gave him directions to the coffee shop next to her apartment. The man looked as pleased as punch. Her good deed was done for the day.

Hannah's ears pricked to the conversation while her eyes stared blankly ahead. A group of women of every shape and size sat in the corner of the usually quiet coffee shop, ignoring their laptops and talking up a storm. The best Hannah could make out, they all belonged to some writing group. Fighting the urge to eavesdrop, Hannah sunk into a plush purple wingback and held her peppermint tea closer to her nose.

As the women discussed salacious plot twists Hannah gave in. She'd always wondered how her favorite writers came up with their ideas. And it would be easier to ignore the stench of coffee than overlook these women.

"But is it romantic or scary? You can't be too careful these days," a redheaded woman said with a slight Southern drawl.

"I'm writing a romance novel, so it has to be romantic," a tiny brunette answered back. "I'm telling you, it was fate. I was sitting here staring at a blank page and overheard him say how he just had to find this woman. A gift from the writing gods."

"It's just not right," the matron of the group said as she stroked the head of a nervous terrier she kept in a papoose. "You said he was a stalker. You might be using some poor woman's demise as inspiration."

The brunette waved her hand in dismissal. "He was too cute to be a stalker."

"I know," the redhead chimed in. "You can write it as a romance and I'll write it as a thriller. Like parallel universes. I hate what I have so far anyway."

"I need inspiration, too. My hero needs a push," the elderly woman said, still petting the dog. Hannah looked away quickly, not daring to be caught eavesdropping.

Some time while she was listening Derek had arrived. *About time.* Hannah checked her watch. Eight minutes late, as if his time were more important than hers.

He made his way toward her with an oversized mug Hannah dreaded would be coffee. She took a long whiff of her tea and braced herself. At least the writing club would get a kick out of him. If some man's urge to find a mystery woman inspired two novels, Derek and his theories would send this group reeling.

"What are your theories on stalkers?" Hannah asked as he sat down opposite her.

Derek froze halfway between sitting and standing. His

eyes were wide as saucers. "What did...why would...?" he stammered before remembering to sit down. "I don't understand."

Hannah shrugged. "I figured you had an opinion on everything." She took a long slow drink of her tea to fight against the wafts of coffee invading her senses. If only it were warmer and she could sit outside.

"Hannah, I'm not sure what you've heard." Derek set his mug down. Definitely coffee, mocha by the looks of it.

Hannah giggled. She actually made the professor uncomfortable. Score one for her. Leaning in, she whispered, "I was just eavesdropping on a conversation. Never mind."

Relief washed over Derek's face. She exchanged pleasantries with him, enjoying his discomfort. He was making this far too easy for her. He was late, too opinionated, and had probably been accused of being a stalker before.

"I've been wondering about something," Hannah said, schooling her face into an aloof expression. "Have you ever looked at adultery from the other side? Why married men are attracted to certain women? Is there a type they go for?" She absently rubbed the side of her mug, hoping she hadn't given herself away too much. She wanted to know what kept bringing these jerks her way.

"There are quite a few studies about women who prefer to be mistresses," Derek said, leaning back in his velvet chair and checking his watch.

Hannah shook her head. "No, I mean what kind of women these men choose to approach. Is there something similar about them?"

Derek sucked in his bottom lip as his eyebrows knit together. After a brief moment he said, "That's a great idea. I'll research it." He snuck a quick look at the door.

We have a winner. The guy was annoying, late, couldn't

even help her, and obviously had somewhere else to be. "Don't let me keep you," she snapped.

"What?" Derek asked, picking up his mug.

"You're very interested in your watch, the door. You know what? I'm going to head off to work." Hannah picked up her purse from by her feet.

"No!" Derek nearly jumped out of his seat. "I…uh… there's something I wanted to ask you."

Just great. A psychologist who couldn't read people. He was going to ask her out again. Hannah took a deep breath and rounded up her best "I'm really busy at work" excuse. He was a friend of Troy's after all, no need to be bitchy. *Yet.*

"Remember that story you were telling me at the party?" Derek asked.

Hannah nodded without bothering to hide her annoyance. Must she talk about this again?

"It's *him!*" Hannah heard the brunette from the writing group squeal. The inspiration for two novels had to be more interesting than Derek. She turned toward the door—and her heart stopped.

Him. It was him, Mr Forgot It Was There. Mr Good Dreams. In the flesh. Molding herself to the back of her chair, she tried to make the wheels turn in her brain. Adulterer. Stalker. Haunter of dreams.

Great job, Hannah, you've gone from bad to worse.

This had better be good. The very last place Mason wanted to find himself after completing his second twenty-four-hour shift of the week was the coffee shop he'd been thrown out of. If this were Derek's idea of a joke, he'd be paying in blood.

Mason quickly made his way past the counter, hoping the barista wouldn't see him. Hearing her gasp as he walked by, he shook his head. This had better be damn good, and it had better be fast because they were probably both about to get the boot. He scanned the room looking for his brother.

"It's *him*!" a woman squealed. Mason turned to see the writing group that met at the shop all staring up at him. They'd all witnessed the embarrassing scene with the manager. Great, now he was a pariah in his own neighborhood.

"Mason, over here." Shifting his glance, he spied Derek sitting in one of two purple chairs by the window.

He made a beeline toward his brother. A week of mornings in the coffee shop had acquainted him with the writers' group. He was not in the mood to get dragged into a conversation with that chatty bunch.

With her back to him a woman rose from the chair facing Derek.

Even before she turned around he knew. Her. It was her. Miss Next Time Take The Ring Off First. Miss Eyes Of A Different Color. Mason took a deep breath, pulling her into his lungs and willing himself to think. Stunning. Sensual. Every man's fantasy. *Good luck, Mason, you finally have your chance.*

As he watched her spin on her heel his whole body came to attention. He met her gaze and grinned. She was even more beautiful than he remembered. Her hair was swept back into a bun with only a few fringes accenting her face. Her bright shining eyes bored holes in his soul. They narrowed into slits as she turned to Derek.

"You know him?" she snapped.

"Yes, I…uh…actually that's…um…" Derek stammered. Mason began to put the pieces together. Derek had found her and called him. This was *damn* good.

Her head whipped back to him as she made a few deductions of her own. "Where's your ring?"

"I'm not married," Mason was relieved to finally have

the chance to say. Turning to Derek, he said, "You haven't told her?"

"I hadn't gotten that far," Derek managed.

"Don't bother, either of you." She reached down for her purse. Mason shot Derek a pleading glance. She would never believe it coming from him. Hell, he could barely believe it. If Derek was going to explain, it had to be now, and fast.

"Look, Hannah, he's never been married," Derek began. "He was wearing the ring for one of my experiments. I hypothesized more women would come on to him if they thought he was married. I told you about my theory, remember."

She paused, but only for a moment. "I did not come on to him! He came on to me."

"I know," Derek continued. "Mason told me what happened. When you told me the story at Troy's party, I put two and two together."

"Why didn't you tell me then?" she asked, pulling on her charcoal-gray peacoat. "Why lure me down here to fill me in? Why fill me in at all? Is this some kind of sick game you two are playing?"

Mason stepped forward. "He didn't tell me anything, Hannah." Hannah, such a pretty name. Soft and strong, like her. "Derek just asked me to meet him here. I wanted you to know the truth. I don't want you thinking I'm some jerk who cheats on his wife."

Her gaze ricocheted between the two men. Hitching her purse higher on her shoulder, she addressed Derek first. "It was wrong of you to lure me here." She then turned an icy gaze on Mason. "Are you stalking me?"

Mason's eyes widened. "What? No! No." He looked around him. Someone must have told her about his run-in with the store manager. "I was just trying to find you again so I could explain. I like you; I want to get to know you better. I was hoping once we cleared things up we could start over."

Hannah huffed a short breath his way. "We're clear. I'm leaving."

"Wait," Derek said. "You're not going to go out with him?"

"No," Hannah said much too quickly.

"But you have to!" One of the women from the writing group butted in.

"You're the one who said he was a stalker!" Hannah said to the woman.

"Honey, if stalkers look like that I'm going to have to get one. You have to at least go out with him," the woman pleaded.

"No, she doesn't," Mason said, stepping toward her.

"She doesn't?" a voice squeaked from the peanut gallery.

Wide-eyed, Hannah looked up at him. He reached out as if in a dream, tucking his fingers underneath her chin, and angled her mouth up to accept his. He brushed his lips softly against hers, wondering if she'd fight him. Her eyelids drifted closed and he let himself taste her. Gently he kissed her, fighting the urge to push and plunder. Her hands crept up his body, her palms flattened against his chest, resting there for a second before she firmly pushed him away.

As her heavily fringed lids fluttered open she said, "I don't know you. You have no right to kiss me."

Cocking his head to the side, he wondered if she was more upset that he'd kissed her, or that he'd stopped. From the way her chest was hitching with every breath, his money was on the latter. Still, she was fighting the attraction.

"That was not a kiss."

"Excuse me? I know when I've been kissed," she said breathily.

"*This* is a kiss." Mason reached for her, molding his hands on either side of her creamy oval face. Energy pulsed through him as he pressed his lips to hers. This was his one chance to assault her senses the way she did to him with just her presence. A physical expression of just how she made him feel. There was no softness this time, no holding back.

He pressed his body against hers, deepening the kiss, demanding she accept him. His lips were firm where hers were pliant. He swallowed her moan as her lips parted, allowing him inside. His head rushed with the refreshing minty taste of her. He seduced her with the kiss. Caressing. Nipping. Inviting. Taking.

When her fingers ran through his hair, he relaxed his grip. Reluctantly, he pulled away and gazed at her expression, eyes closed, lips still parted. He grinned down at her as her eyes flickered open, the dichotomy of a single blue and a single green eye studying him intently. Derek was an idiot with his ideas about symmetry. The play of the two colors against each other was amazingly sexy.

"That was a kiss," she whispered, licking her lips.

CHAPTER THREE

CLIMBING down the ladder in her kitten heels, Hannah set the armload of negligees on the rolling cart. She was going to strangle whatever genius thought to top-stock hanging lingerie. *Right before the holiday season.* As if the floor staff needed a reason not to rotate the aisle presentations.

Straightening her gray sheath dress, Hannah pushed the cart out the swinging doors of the stockroom and onto the sales floor. Most of the year she tried to appeal to women, but during the holiday she wanted to turn a man's head. Taking the sheer ivory gown from the mannequin, she replaced it with a pink baby-doll flyaway trimmed in black lace. She stepped back to admire the handiwork and hoped it would interest a man. It had been so long since she'd been with one she wasn't sure. Would Mason prefer satin, sheer, lace, or nothing at all?

"Fine Jewelry Two, Fine Jewelry Two," the intercom paged. Staffing was light so Hannah pushed the cart to the back room and headed over to the jewelry counter.

Hannah gave a "can I help you?" smile to a perky brunette eyeing the bridal sets. After trying on a few, the woman settled on one, and turned to look for her fiancé.

"Honey, look at this one," she chirped as the blond man approached the counter and stopped Hannah's heart cold.

Marty.

He had the nerve to be in her store? Granted when they had been together she'd started working on the Westside, but still. Careless bastard should have known better.

Sucking in a deep breath, Hannah straightened her posture, forced a smile and looked him in the eye. She recognized terror as he tugged the woman's arm from the counter.

"Excuse me." Hannah's voice rang out as clear as a bell. "The ring?" She held her hand open in expectation.

"Martin!" the woman chided, sidling back to the counter. "You said we'd get the ring today."

"Not here," Marty snapped, his face reddening.

"You said today." The woman pouted.

"He must have somewhere to go," Hannah taunted, surprising herself with the pleasure of finally having power over the jerk. He couldn't expect her to let him get away with this.

Marty's eyes narrowed as he looked at her. *Simple brown eyes.* What she'd ever seen in them she didn't know. Broadening her grin, Hannah decided to have some fun. "At least you'll save some money."

"Oh, is there a special sale today?" the woman asked hopefully.

Hannah shook her head and addressed Marty again. "Marty's pockets are full of gold, aren't they, Marty?"

He grabbed the woman's arm and gave it a not-so-gentle tug. "We're leaving. Now."

Hannah caught the hand still wearing the ring. The woman was caught in the middle of a cruel tug-of-war. Hannah released her first, remembering how she'd felt when she'd first discovered his deception.

"Ouch!" the woman yelped, removing the ring and returning it to Hannah. "I take it you two know each other."

Marty's glare shot daggers at her, but she didn't care.

Hannah lowered her voice and looked the woman in the eye. "Honey, he won't buy you a ring. He's married, with three kids."

She arrived early. Mason smiled from his perch in the bar, watching as she made her way into the restaurant. He hated to be kept waiting. Especially for something he'd looked so forward too.

She looked amazing. Her soft brown hair fell loosely across her back. He liked it down, long and flowing and begging to be touched. He wanted to touch her so badly his hands balled into fists at his sides.

Dropping a few bills on the bar, he slid off his stool. In just a few long strides he found himself beside her, helping her off with her coat. He indulged himself, allowing his fingers to brush against her hair. Softer than he'd imagined, like spun silk.

Her scent wafted through him. It was a light floral scent, fresh like flowers after the rain. How had he missed that before? Had the aroma of detergent or coffee simply washed her scent out, or had she put it on tonight for him?

Pulling her coat away from her body he stepped back, and allowed himself a long, lingering gaze. She was exquisite from head to toe. Her wide-neck sweater kissed at her creamy shoulders. The hazy pale gray of the sweater complemented her eyes. He was fascinated by the angle of her collarbone, the curve of her neck, the little dip where her throat met her torso. The neck of her sweater was too high to gift him with a view of cleavage, but he drank in the swells of her breasts beneath the delicate fabric.

His gaze drifted down her body, enjoying the silky look of the black skirt twirling a few inches above her knee. The black tights she wore were disappointing, but the boots made him want to beg for mercy. A toe so pointy it must be painful. Black leather laced up the side all the way to her knee. The thin heel on the boots was at least three inches high. *Yowza.*

"Mason?" Her sweet voice snapped him back to reality.

He cleared his throat, twice, before even trying to say something coherent. "Hmm?" was all he could manage with all the blood in his body occupied south of the border.

"I asked if you'd been waiting long. I know how much I hate to be kept waiting."

With those boots, she almost looked him in the eye. If he wanted to kiss her he could just lean forward. A genius must have designed those things.

"You're not much of a talker, are you?" she asked, cocking her head to the side.

He cleared his throat again but before he spoke a hostess arrived, leading them to their table. Why Hannah had chosen this restaurant, he'd never know. Orchid was a popular Thai place, more family than romantic. But it was just two blocks from the laundromat. Maybe she wanted to stick close to home.

"Do you like living downtown?" he managed to ask after cooling his body temperature with the ice water the hostess set before him.

Her posture straightened. "How do you know where I live?"

Mason held open his hands. "I don't. I just assumed. This place, the laundromat and the coffee shop are all within a three-block radius. Something is pulling you this direction."

Her expression softened as she relaxed her shoulders. "You shouldn't assume. All three places are close to the train line as well."

He smiled and shook his head. "You're never going to cut me a break, are you?"

"Not until you've earned it." She grinned back, taking a sip from her own glass. Her ripe mouth mesmerized Mason. As her pink tongue darted between her full lips to swipe a stray drop of water he widened his legs, allowing more room in his pants. He knew all too vividly the things she might manage with that tongue.

Mason drained the rest of his water, rattling the ice cubes in the bottom of the glass. After wiping the condensation from the glass he spread the cool water across the back of his neck. Was she really making him sweat? By sheer proximity? If she could do this completely clothed he'd be wrecked if she were naked. A vision of her naked danced before his eyes, making him grab the edge of the table. He had to get a grip on something.

"Do you like spicy?" Hannah asked from behind her menu. She certainly wasn't going to let up. "The hotter the better."

The man got hotter every time she saw him. Before he'd always been wearing work clothes. She'd wondered if it was the fire-department emblem that made him so sexy. Hannah had always had a thing for heroes. But it wasn't the uniform that turned her head; it was the man beneath it.

Hannah was impressed to see he'd primped a bit himself. His work boots were replaced by brushed leather Oxfords. Her gaze rested on the V of his broad chest, covered in soft blue cashmere. The fabric draped suggestively, reminding her of the body she dreamed about beneath. The cobalt of the sweater brought out the pinstripe in the flat-front microfiber slacks he wore. His warm brown hair was still spiky, but less "just rolled out of bed" and more natural and touchable.

And she wanted to touch him. Every long inch of him, while staring into those deep middle-of-the-ocean-blue eyes. It was now officially her favorite color.

Hannah needed to get a grip on herself. She'd agonized over what to wear for almost an hour before copying the outfit on a mannequin she'd dressed yesterday. She'd changed, let her hair down and spritzed herself with perfume all before leaving the store. Everyone must have known she was going on a date.

The sick thing was, she'd wanted them to. Everyone at work teased her for being a workaholic. This was her first actual date in a long time. Something she'd planned beforehand and made time for. This was the first date she'd been on during the holiday season in four years.

Which had probably made things very easy for Marty, she thought with a huff. Maybe married men scoped out retail managers because they would be too busy to notice you ignoring them during one of the most important times of the year. She shook her head to dispel the memory. He had no business here, tonight.

"What?" Mason's low baritone rumbled over the hum of the restaurant.

"What what?" she teased up at him as she smiled. He had the bluest eyes she'd ever seen. A true cobalt-blue, she noticed in the bright fluorescent lighting of the restaurant.

"You shook your head," Mason said wistfully. "My conversational skills disappointing you again?"

"Of course not," Hannah said, reaching her hand across the table. "You were a little quiet in the beginning, but you warmed right up. I'm actually relieved dominating a conversation isn't a family trait."

In the last half-hour, they'd covered all the first-date basics. Hannah had discovered they actually had a lot in common. They liked the same music, generally, the same style of furniture, occasionally, and had very similar tastes in books. They had rambled about everything and nothing as they'd made their way through appetizers and entrées.

There was nothing about him she hated, a lot of things she liked. He was very good at listening, waiting for her to volunteer information instead of prying it out of her. Something was happening with this man, something wonderful.

She laid her fingers lightly over his, amazed by the warmth of his skin. Every inch of this man was hot. Too tempting. She hadn't even figured out what was wrong with him yet. Hannah pulled her hand back.

Flipping his hand over, he caught hers, blocking her retreat with the steady grasp of his fingers. Palm to palm, the heat pulsing between them was impossible to ignore. His thumb slowly rubbed across the back of her hand. The contrast of textures made her all the more aware the casual touch was anything but.

"Do you want to know why?" His expression changed. No longer free and easy, he was suddenly serious.

"Are you going to give me a lesson on genetics?" she teased to lighten his mood. She was still too nervous with him to go there. "Are all firemen experts on the rules of inheritance?"

He shook his head slowly as a grin played on his lips. "Firefighter. Firemen are the guys who load coal on trains."

"What?"

"Nothing, it's just a reflex. You look amazing."

"Thank you," she said automatically, deflecting the compliment by looking away. Heat prickled her from her shoulders to her cheeks. *Blushing.* As if she'd done something wrong. She felt the weight of his stare on her bare shoulders and she swung her hair forward. She tried to remove her hand but he held firm, his thumb continuing a lazy circle of the back of her hand.

"Hannah." Mason's voice rumbled between them.

Her stomach fluttered. She still wasn't used to the sound

of her name on his lips. She wasn't shy, just out of practice, she reminded herself. There was no need to act like an inexperienced schoolgirl, no matter how he was making her swoon. After all, this was exactly the reaction she'd hoped to get from him when she'd bought this outfit this afternoon. She looked up to meet his gaze.

"When I saw you I couldn't think, just like the first time. You're beautiful." He smiled, the dimple in his left cheek making a token appearance. "And those boots are doing terrible things to my self-control."

Hannah's tongue pushed against the back of her teeth as she smiled in glee. She was affecting *his* self-control? At least that leveled the playing field. "They are fantastic, aren't they?" She jutted a long leg from beneath the table. "We just got them in last night. They're completely impractical, but too fantastic to resist."

"I can think of some practical uses for them." Mason's fingers wrapped around her wrist. If he took her pulse right now he might guess what she was thinking. Him on his knees, her standing in front of him wearing nothing but the come-and-get-me boots. He would look up at her with an expression not unlike the one he'd worn when they'd started down this road—*too far, too fast*.

She jerked her hand back as if she'd been bitten. She was not going to be seduced by someone she didn't know ever again.

"You could aerate a lawn," he offered quietly. Her eyes searched him as he slowly withdrew his hand across the table.

"That's really what you were thinking?" she heard herself taunt. She might be out of practice when it came to dating, but she knew a come-on when she heard one. Or at least she thought she did.

He grinned across the table. "No, but given your reaction

it seemed like a nice save." A waiter returned with their bill. Tucking her hair behind her ears, she reminded herself the naughty vision lived in her own head. She shouldn't punish Mason for her overactive, undersexed imagination.

After Mason dealt with the waiter, he turned his attention back to Hannah. "I was thinking in those boots you wouldn't have to stand on your toes to kiss me." He rose from his chair. "Shall we?" he asked, offering her his hand.

"Kiss? Here?" In the middle of a crowded restaurant? Had he forgotten how she'd reacted the last time he'd kissed her? Hannah's stomach quivered at the thought and she licked her lips in anticipation. She remembered all too well the delicious kisses this man served up, and she very much wanted to sample some more.

Mason laughed wickedly and shook his head, pulling her to her feet. Her body pressed against his on impact. Her nipples peaked immediately as his hard chest pressed against hers. "Any time, anywhere. But I was thinking I'd walk you home first."

Mason held Hannah's hand as they crossed the street. Innocent enough, gentlemanly even, if not for the ever-present tickle of his finger against her palm. A tickle that intensified as it made its way straight to her core.

Stopping short, he jerked his arm forward, propelling Hannah into his open arms. Wrapping her against him, he whispered, "Wait for me. Let me surprise you."

She was so surprised by the way he whirled her around she was out of breath. All she could do was nod. His lips brushed her cheek as he released her, disappearing into a candy shop.

Hannah forced herself not to stare in the shop window, drooling after him. Instead she turned her attention to the display window of the neighboring store.

She decided headless mannequins made for a more attractive presentation. The painted faces and tacky wigs distracted from the clothes and accessories. Hannah admired the snub-toe tweed pumps in the display, studying them hopefully.

"Hannah?" a man's voice said from behind her. Not Mason's. Hannah looked into the reflection of the window. Jeremy Tolliver, one of the other store-manager candidates. Fixing a smile on her face, she turned around.

"Jeremy, what a surprise," she said, not bothering to mask her lack of enthusiasm.

He nodded, his gaze traveling up and down and up again. *Pig.* "I tried to call you today, but you'd already left."

"Really?" she said, feigning interest. "Did you lose your buyer directory again?"

Jeremy gave a strangled laugh. "No, I wanted to talk to you about the management training seminar. I offered to help you lead it."

Hannah was careful not to let her surprise show. The seminars were complete and ready to go. Several days next week devoted to traveling to the different stores in the metro area and rallying the management teams to holiday greatness.

"The seminar for your store? Your input would be helpful. We can target your newer managers directly."

Jeremy shook his head. "All of the stores. Dean and Judy agreed you need the help."

She was thankful for the heels on her boots as she met his leering gaze. He'd talked to the district and regional managers about her needing help? She schooled her face into a polite smile. She didn't need anyone's help, least of all a chubby deadweight like Jeremy Tolliver.

"We'll be spending a lot of time together," Jeremy continued, stepping closer.

Where the hell was Mason? Jeremy had made passes at

her before, but she'd always been able to deflect with humor or quotations from the Mendelssohn's employee handbook. If Jeremy stepped any closer Hannah might find another practical use for the heel of her new boots.

"Give me a call tomorrow at work and we can discuss how you want to contribute." She knew Jeremy well enough to know he was looking for credit, not extra work. She'd give him the kudos if he'd leave her the hell alone.

"Let's grab a cup of coffee and talk about it now. Or not talk about it." He tilted his head downward. She saw no redeeming flecks of color in his black eyes.

"I'm actually waiting for someone." Hannah backed against the glass. She took a deep breath and reminded herself she had to work with this guy. She'd be paying for bitchy brush-offs for years, especially if she wound up managing his store.

"I don't believe that." His voice lowered. "No man in his right mind would leave you all alone."

Hannah squared her shoulders. Bitchy it was.

"I am a little bit crazy." She heard Mason's rich baritone drawl as his fingers slipped around her clenched fist. Hannah enjoyed every twitch of Jeremy's face as the two men eyed each other. Handing the silver bag he carried to her, Mason stuck out his hand. "Mason McNally. And you are?"

Jeremy returned the gesture. "Jeremy Tolliver. Hannah and I work very closely together."

"Oh, Jeremy." Mason turned and gave her a knowing look. "Right, Hannah's mentioned you."

Hannah fought the grin playing at her lips. Mason played his role very effectively.

Jeremy scowled at Mason. "I just asked Hannah about going for coffee. Why don't you join us?"

Mason looked quizzically down at the other man. He was smiling, almost laughing. "Hannah doesn't drink coffee." He shook his head slightly and made a move to check his watch. Without actually looking at the time, he went on, "It's getting late. I need to get Hannah to bed. She has to be at work early tomorrow. Nice meeting you."

Hannah graced Jeremy with a smile as she gladly took Mason's hand and let him lead her away.

Once they were out of earshot Mason asked, "Did I blow that? I guessed from the peppermint tea yesterday you don't drink coffee, right?"

"No, you were right. Talking about me as if I wasn't standing next to you was strange, but I'm glad you were there." As she squeezed his hand he stopped walking and turned her to face him.

"That guy gives me the creeps."

Hannah rolled her eyes. "Try working with him."

"I mean it, Hannah, I don't like the way he was looking at you." Mason's thumb played with the back of her hand as he spoke.

Hannah forced a laugh to lighten the mood. "It's a little early for you to be getting all possessive on me, don't you think?"

Pursing his lips into a thin line, Mason nodded. Not exactly the brevity she was going for.

"I'm still waiting." She tried again.

Mason's eyebrow arched quizzically, then he smiled. "Oh, right. Your surprise." Taking and opening the silver bag, he dug out a tiny silver box and opened that. Two chocolate truffles shone in the light from the street lamps. "Try it. This one first." He pointed to the chocolate dome in front decorated with shimmering gold flecks.

Hannah balanced the candy between her fingers and took a bite. She offered the other half to Mason. The candy fell into his mouth but he caught her wrist, sending shivers up her spine as he sucked the melted chocolate from her fingertips.

The truffle melted in her mouth. The rich, sweet sensation grew as her mouth heated. Somehow it was hot without being spicy, sweet without being sugary.

"Is there chili in that?" she asked, savoring the last effects of the treat on her tongue.

Mason nodded and stepped closer. "I guessed from dinner you like things hot."

Did she ever. "What if I hadn't offered to share?"

Mason leaned in, licking her lips gently. Her stomach tightened in anticipation. As she parted her lips in invitation he went further, sucking her bottom lip between his before kissing her fully.

She loved the flavor of the candy, but the feel of him melting with the taste of chocolate was exhilarating. There was something about the clean way he smelled and the taste of him melding with the heat from the chili chocolate that made her moan. He pulled away too quickly, leaving Hannah feeling she'd somehow been short-changed.

As her eyes fluttered open she realized she wasn't done with him. This man made kissing an art form, and she wanted to learn every nuance of his technique. She reached for him, but he stepped back. "Try the other one."

What she wanted right now wasn't chocolate, it was him. But as she came to her senses and the world widened she realized eating chocolate was a much more appropriate activity for a busy sidewalk. She reached into the box and removed the plain chocolate cube. Staring into Mason's eyes, she popped the whole thing in her mouth.

As the truffle melted she was overcome with the cool sensation. It wasn't just mint, but peppermint. Her favorite. She eyed him as she rolled the flavors over her tongue. He couldn't possibly have planned it, but she would love to give him credit for it anyway. Extra credit.

"Are you going to share?" Mason whispered, gently brushing his lips across hers. A laugh hummed through her as the kiss began. She loved the firm feel of his demanding lips on hers. The taste of the chocolates and him mingled with his masculine scent and sent colors dancing across her closed eyelids.

Somewhere far away she heard the bag drop as his hands came up to cup her face. As he introduced her to his tongue her knees weakened and she brought her hands to his chest for support. Her hands reflexively squeezed the rock-hard pecs beneath the soft sweater. She should take up sculpting; this man's body was a work of art. She wished she weren't wearing a coat so she could press her body against his and feel every inch of him.

She inhaled deeply, releasing her breath in a long sigh, and drew away slightly, just enough to look into his eyes. She touched his face, her finger tracing the lips she had just savored. Pleasure propelled her forward as she caught the smell of his skin and began swathing him with soft, gentle kisses once more.

A whistle from another place and time echoed in her ears. Mason pulled away slowly, then stepped back, out of reach. Hannah reached a hand to her own mouth, amazed at the sensation. If he kissed like that, Hannah ached to know what else he could do.

CHAPTER FOUR

"YOU'VE got to be kidding me," Mason said when they came to a stop in front of the apartment building.

"What?" Hannah asked, turning and stepping in front of him without releasing his hand. "You have a problem with my building?"

He shook his head and laughed. "I live here."

"You've got to be kidding me," Hannah echoed.

"I moved in two months ago." Mason reached forward and grabbed her free hand, squeezing them both. "4B. How did I miss you?"

Hannah shrugged her shoulders. "I work a lot."

So much for maintaining a safe distance and taking her goodnight kiss on the sidewalk. Pursing her lips together, Hannah looked deep in his eyes and quieted the niggling voice in the back of her mind that cautioned her with safe-dating rules. The voice that reminded her an entire coffee shop thought he was stalking her. She trusted him. At least as far as her door.

"Shall we?" Mason punched the code and opened the door to the small lobby.

"Since you live above me, I guess I don't have to invite you up," Hannah said, entering the warm building. "Do you mind?" she motioned to the row of mailboxes. "I haven't checked the mail yet today."

"I haven't checked mine all week." Mason laughed.

As they opened their locked mailboxes Hannah noted his was just four away. She flipped through her mail, glad it was relatively benign. A fashion magazine, two catalogs, the electric bill, and a card from her mother. "Trade ya," she teased, looking at Mason's hefty pile.

"Any time you want to pay my bills, you're welcome to them," he said without looking up.

Hannah stepped closer. He had at least five magazines. "You must like to read."

"I like to fantasize."

Rolling her eyes, Hannah peeked at the titles. Not a girlie magazine in the stack. He did seem to have an extreme sports fetish though. When did he find the time to backpack, snow-board, sea-kayak and scuba-dive?

"You see anything you like?" he teased, offering the stack to her.

It was too tempting an offer to refuse from someone she knew so little about. Taking the stack from him, she handed him her own.

"Hannah, I was kidding," he said as she rifled through the envelopes. Mostly bills and junk mail. Two envelopes caught her attention. Both were large and thick, hand addressed on high-quality paper. She held them up. "Two wedding invitations?"

"How can you tell from the envelope?" He plucked them from her hand. After checking the return addresses on the backs he said, "My frat brothers seem to have all decided to get married this year. I missed the memo."

"I'm so glad I didn't join a sorority." Hannah returned his stack of mail. "You must go broke having to buy all those gifts."

Mason smiled. "The gifts are no problem. It's when they

make you wear a tux and dance with the bridesmaids that I start to get annoyed."

"You're in those weddings?"

He shrugged. "One of them, yeah. It's my third this year. Like I said, there was a memo." He paused as they neared the staircase. "Come with me."

Hannah stopped mid-step. "That's sweet, Mason, but you don't have to do that."

"Do what?" he asked, bounding up the stairs.

"It's our first date. Wedding invitations are sent out months in advance."

He looked down at her from the first landing. "Gabe's is New Year's Eve. As crazy as your schedule is, that will probably be the next time I see you."

Hannah smiled, wishing that weren't so on the mark. "A New Year's Eve wedding sounds romantic," she said, beginning the treacherous climb in her stiletto boots.

Mason waited for her on the second floor. "You'd think so, but Gabe's an accountant. He wanted the date for the tax write-off." They laughed and fell in step beside one another, making it to the third floor.

Mason stared at the number on her door. "3B. You live right beneath me."

Hannah nodded, standing in front of her door with her keys in one hand and her mail in the other. An alarm in her head reminded her this was their first date. A kiss at the door would be the smart thing, but she wanted more than a kiss. Not much more, but a little. She wanted him to touch her, to be able to touch him. And since it had been her brilliant idea to check the mail on the way up—

"You're deciding, aren't you?"

"Deciding what?" She knew she was being coy, but she hadn't made up her mind yet.

"Whether or not to ask me in."

She stared at him, the moment becoming heavy and charged with emotion. She wanted him. Wanted him to come in, kiss her, make love to her until dawn.

The last one was what she was afraid of.

She wondered if she had it in her to do casual sex. People did it all the time. And with as long as it had been, and as good as he looked, she wanted to do it right now.

She put the key in the lock. Turning it slowly, she decided she wouldn't sleep with him. But a girl could play.

He followed her in, stepping on an envelope. "You must have dropped this," he said, handing it to her.

"I don't think so." She flipped it over. "It's not even addressed. It must be from one of the neighbors. It's not even sealed." Pushing back the flap, she pulled out a card with a picture of a Christmas tree on the front. She opened it and saw it was blank inside. "Well, that's odd. They must have forgotten to sign it."

She moved to set it on the table, but Mason took it from her hand. His eyebrows knit together as he studied the front of the card. He looked at Hannah beneath his lowered brows.

"I don't want to scare you, but did you look at this tree?"

"What?" She took the card back. It was an innocuous-looking Douglas fir, decorated for the holiday. As she peered closer she realized what he saw. Instead of a paper chain wrapping around the tree, this one had handcuffs linked together.

"What do you make of it?" Hannah spoke into the phone while she peeled the plastic bags from her dry-cleaning.

"We have a kinky neighbor," her roommate, Kate, replied. "We could regift it since it's unsigned. If I knew someone who would appreciate the humor of handcuffs on a Christmas tree. You probably would have better luck. Don't you feel enslaved by the season?"

"Energized. It's the best time to be in retail." Hannah meant every word.

"If it freaked you out, I'll come home this weekend and walk the halls without my makeup on."

"Come home if you want, but I doubt you'll see me. I have this weekend to get my departments set and prep for the training seminars." Which she'd thought was done, but Jeremy Tolliver's new add-on sales ideas had her scrambling to give him time to present.

She still didn't understand why the brass even gave him a shot at a district-wide program with his plan. It sounded like a lot of busy work to Hannah, who wanted to focus on keeping morale high. Higher employee satisfaction meant a lower absentee rate and higher employee retention. With a sigh Hannah put her busy thoughts aside. She'd already given thirteen hours to the store today.

"You're a workaholic." Hannah could hear Kate clicking her pen in the background.

"Right back at you babe." She lined up her outfits for the week in the closet. It was so much easier to get dressed at four in the morning when you didn't have to think about what you were putting on.

"You're really not going to tell me." Kate quieted her pen.

"Tell you what?"

"About your date! I'm stuck in K-Falls with no prospects. Let me live through you a little."

Hannah did the highlight reel for Kate, omitting Mason's anxiety about the card. And that he'd made it inside the apartment. Kate would be even more disappointed than Hannah at how the card had ruined the mood of the evening.

His protective side had come out, and, as attractive as it was, it had killed any thoughts Hannah had of sleeping with him. Mason was more boyfriend material than one-night stand.

"When are you seeing him again?" Kate asked with a sigh.

"Not for a while. I need to focus on work, then I have the training seminars and I still have my departments to run. Which is why I never date during holiday." Lying back on her bed, Hannah glanced at the clock. Eight-thirty and already so tired she was dressed for bed. Thank goodness she closed tomorrow and didn't have to be in until after lunch.

"Exactly how long is a while?"

"I have next Thursday off so he's going to see if he can work his schedule so we can spend the day together."

The rap at the door had her sitting bolt upright. Her heart beat in her throat. She hadn't buzzed anyone up. The card had her more on edge than she'd realized.

"Somebody's here." She rose from the bed and flipped on the lights as she made her way across the living room and to the door. She peered through the peephole. "Mason," she breathed into the phone.

"He's there? Stop wasting time with me, honey. One of us needs to get a little action."

Clicking off the phone, Hannah looked down and cursed her sister. Molly always gave her things from the upscale lingerie store she managed. Really great things Hannah couldn't resist.

"Just a minute," Hannah called as she scurried to her bedroom and grabbed a robe to cover the sage-green stretch-lace chemise she wore. Hannah loved lingerie, but wasn't sure she wanted Mason to know just how much yet. He'd definitely get the wrong idea, she thought as she cinched the belt on the ivory satin robe.

She took a quick look in the bathroom mirror on the way

to the door and cursed herself for having washed her makeup off already.

Hannah opened the door slowly, hiding her body behind its bulk.

"I tried to call, but your line was busy." Mason stayed in the doorway. "I got my schedule for next month and I wanted to check it with yours before I volunteer for extra shifts."

Hannah smiled. He looked so good just standing there in his work clothes. Judging by the duffle bag at his feet he'd come straight from work, not even bothering to stop in upstairs.

Why was it she looked at him standing there and felt her temperature rise, her stomach tighten? Could he possibly be just that sexy? She opened the door wider but he stayed in the hall. "Do you want to come in or discuss it here?"

"I didn't want to assume." He dropped his bag inside the doorway and stepped inside. She crossed the room and powered up her organizer so they could compare calendars. Turning, she watched him swallow hard. Twice.

"Are you thirsty? I have wine and soda, Kate has four kinds of vodka in the freezer." She smiled at that last one. Mason drinking green-apple-flavored vodka was a funny thought. Though she didn't know what he drank.

"Did you know I was coming?" he asked, his voice raspy and dry.

"No. Why?" He'd barely stepped into the room.

"Are you seeing someone else? I know we've only been on one date, but I thought you were single." His eyes were carefully fixed on hers.

"Mason, I can hardly find the time to date you. How am I going to juggle someone else?" Hannah sat on the corduroy sofa and clicked the pen over her electronic organizer until December's calendar came up.

"Do you always dress like this when you're home alone? You are alone, right?"

Hannah searched his face, grinning at her own power. She made him nervous. Maybe she shouldn't have put on the robe. She could probably have him begging right now.

"This is how I dress for bed." Her voice came out lower than usual, slower. She watched his Adam's apple bob as he swallowed again. Given the current state of his pants, Hannah felt pretty confident she could have him naked and in her bed in less than sixty seconds if she played her cards right. But she wasn't sure if she wanted to be in the game just yet.

She looked down at her calendar. December was better than November: she had three days off. "I've got the second, twenty-fifth, and thirty-first." Her birthday, Christmas, and New Year's Eve.

"Right, the schedule." Mason bent down and rifled through his duffle, pulling out a printed sheet of paper and a pen. He stepped closer to the couch, but hesitated before sitting down.

"Relax, Mason, I won't bite." She patted the couch next to her, squeezing her thighs together in anticipation. She already sensed the smell of soap and aftershave and man that she'd memorized just last night.

"It's not you I'm worried about," he said under his breath as he sat down. He circled her days off on his calendar. "I actually have all of those. Okay, what else?"

Looking up, he met her gaze and her breath caught. His eyes were so blue it almost hurt to look at them. "That's it. I warned you the holidays were crazy. But if you stick it out they give you a week off in February." She smiled and searched the schedule for any days when she could get off early and not be in until closing the next day.

"Did you take New Year's Eve off for Gabe's wedding?"

She considered lying, but shook her head. "I actually paid a hundred bucks for it in a United Way fundraiser."

He smiled, his straight teeth gleaming. "Will you come with me to the wedding?"

New Year's was still a long way off. "If you're still speaking to me, absolutely."

"I'll make you a deal. You always answer the door dressed like this and I will until the day I die."

Her laugh was louder than she would've liked. "If you like the robe you should have seen what I was wearing when you knocked." His pupils dilated, his irises darkening at her taunt. She was playing with fire here. She looked away, studying the schedule once more. "I could do dinner on the eighth or nineteenth if you want."

He bowed his head again. "I work on the eighth, but I'm in for the nineteenth. You probably have family stuff on Christmas so what about the second? Do you ski?"

"Yes, but no. The second is my birthday and my folks are flying in. We do our family thing then, so my sisters can be with their in-laws for Christmas."

"Birthday?" He grinned, that charming dimple appearing.

She wanted to ignore her thirtieth birthday altogether. "Did you get Thursday off?"

"I think so. I have to trade some December days, but I wanted to check with you first."

"Good answer." She smiled, turning off her organizer and setting it on the coffee-table.

"I read that book," Mason said, setting down his calendar. He'd circled her days off and noted her birthday.

"What book?" she wondered, looking up at him.

"*Just One Night.*" He scooted closer until their bodies touched from hip to knee. Even his body temperature was hot.

"*Just One Night*? My romance novel? The one I was reading when we met?"

"Uh-huh." His voice dropped an octave as his fingers twirled a lock of her hair.

Just like in the book. Every nerve in her body came alive. "Oh, my God. You're thinking about when they…"

"Oh, yes," he said, leaning toward her, breathing in the smell of her hair. Just as the cowboy did when he found the heroine asleep in his bed.

"I can't," she whispered, feeling her body betray her words. Her mouth watered, her nipples hardened, an ache throbbed between her thighs.

"Please." Bursts of soft breath tickled her ears, warming her from within.

His warm, wet tongue explored the winding curves of her ear. At first lightly nibbling, and then sucking her earlobe. Her breath stuttered in her throat. How was it no matter where he touched, she felt it between her legs?

"She was asleep," she somehow managed to say. Not much of an argument against what he wanted, what they both wanted, but the best she could come up with.

He pulled away abruptly, making Hannah gasp at his absence. "You're right. Go." He motioned toward the hall. "I'll wait."

"You'll wait." Hannah watched as he leaned back on the couch, crossing his thick arms over his broad chest. *Could she wait?* Could she ever fall asleep knowing he would wake her with his mouth?

Mason nodded slowly, sending chills down her spine with every move of his head. Her blood somehow thickened, making every beat of her heart thunder in her ears. *How she wanted this man.* But her rational brain had not completely shut down. She shouldn't be doing this.

"I'd never be able to fall asleep, knowing you were out here, waiting to wake me."

The dimple appeared in his left cheek. "So pretend."

It was too soon. Too soon to want him this badly. Too soon to trust him that much. No matter how tempting his sexy offer.

"I love it when you do that." He smiled, shifting on the couch to face her. "It's like there are two parts of you fighting it out. One eyebrow goes up and then the other. It is sexy as hell."

She laughed at his observation. He was scoring points with her now.

He leaned closer. "So who wins—blue or green?"

"What?" she asked, cocking her head to the side.

"That's how I think of it. Your blue eye battling your green."

Now he was calling her a freak. Her face fell as she straightened her posture. She would not let it bother her.

"What did I say?"

"Forget it." She crossed her arms over her chest.

His hand moved to her knee. "You have to tell me so I don't do it again. I knew tonight was a long shot, but you can't blame me for trying. I mean, look at you."

She took a deep breath. She didn't want it to happen again either. "I can be a little over-sensitive about my eyes. I used to wear contacts to fix them, but they're part of who I am, you know."

"What's wrong with your eyes?" His expression filled with concern.

Humor seemed the way to go. "Mason, I don't know how to break this to you, but they're two different colors."

He went from smiling to puzzled to smiling again. "In case you don't recall, your eyes were the first things I liked about you. Really liked, actually." He shook his head. "I can't believe you would poke yourself in the eye to hide them."

Hannah shrugged. "Kids can be cruel." And mothers who wanted their daughters to be perfect. Hannah's eyes had always embarrassed her mother, who had started putting a contact lens in her left eye when Hannah was only six.

"Which one did you pick?" he asked, the lamplight dancing in his eyes.

"Which one what?" She felt him studying her eyes intently, but she wouldn't let herself look away.

"When you went for one color, which way did you go?"

"Blue. It was easier to match. Why?"

"Just trying to figure out my odds tonight." He rubbed the silky material of her robe between his fingers.

"Not good, I'm afraid. Is that why you came?" She did and didn't want to know the answer.

He shook his head. "I won't wait until next Thursday to see you again." He let the statement hang in the air between them. She didn't want to wait an entire week either, but between her schedule and his there wasn't much they could do about it. The thought of not kissing him for an entire week stabbed at her.

A low chuckle came more from his chest than his throat.

"What's funny?" she asked the top of his head. He was intent on studying her thigh. Right where her robe came open, revealing the hem of her chemise. She fought the urge to pull her robe closed.

"It's even the same green as your eye. The part of you you're willing to hide." His hand slid up her knee, caressing her thigh, not stopping until he grasped her hip. The nerve endings there exploded, making her tingle from elbow to knee and everywhere in between.

"Mason," she whispered in warning as he leaned closer.

"You look so beautiful. I'll do anything you want, Hannah, or nothing at all. If you change your mind I swear I'll stop. Just tell me when."

CHAPTER FIVE

"WHEN." Hannah's lips quivered, her voice barely audible.

"I mean it," Mason said, brushing his lips back and forth against hers. "But if you want me to stop I'll have to go."

If he left he would have to stop that slow circle around her hip his thumb was tracing. She didn't want that to ever stop. Slowly her eyes opened as she stared into his. Could he stop? Did he actually believe he could? Because she wasn't sure she had that kind of control.

"I want you too, but it's too soon." Her rejection didn't register in his eyes.

"It doesn't feel rushed at all, does it?"

He was right. Sitting there, breathing his breath felt like the most perfect thing in the world.

Without taking his eyes from hers he undid the belt of her robe, spreading it open and off her shoulders. His eyes showed his lust, but there was something more that made her decision for her. There was an awe, almost a reverence and he wasn't even looking at her body.

"I don't want *Just One Night*," she whispered, shrugging the robe off her shoulders.

"You have me booked for the next month and a half." His gaze drifted south.

Hannah smiled, liking the sound of all that implied. Threading her fingers through his hair, she pulled him closer. "I meant I don't want it to be like the book. I want it to be you and me."

She traced his lips with her tongue, her arousal building as she heard his breath hitch. Taking his bottom lip between her own, she sucked gently, pulling him into the kiss. She kissed him as she'd always wanted to. The way she did in her dreams, without holding anything back, finally finding an outlet for the passion burning inside.

Holding her shoulders in his hands, Mason pulled away slowly. The only solace Hannah took in the separation was that he had even more trouble controlling his breathing than she did. Pressing his forehead against hers, he ground his teeth together and said, "I don't have anything with me. I swear, I will sprint up those stairs if you will hold that thought."

Hannah smiled at his candor. "You really didn't plan this?"

He shook his head. "Your outfit inspired me to aim high."

They laughed together, his fingers running beneath the lacy straps of her chemise. "Bedroom." Her voice came out lower, throatier than ever before.

"Okay," Mason said, getting up slowly. "I'll be right back."

Rising, Hannah shook her head and took his hand. "Now."

How Mason loved a modern woman. She led him back through the hall and into her bedroom, switching off the lights as she made her way. He would have preferred them on, but there would be time to talk her into that later.

Turning the corner into her bedroom, he lengthened his stride, making it to the bed before her and pulling her down with him. Rolling on top of her, he tried to kiss her but she turned her head, denying him.

"That's not how I want to play." Hannah was limp beneath him.

"No?" He rolled to the far side of the double bed.

"No," she said, rising up and moving over to straddle him. She really was every man's fantasy. "And here I thought I was trying to seduce you," he managed to say, ignoring the heat coming off her body. It had been a long time, far too long for him to blow it now.

"Did you really?" she asked, unbuttoning his shirt. He lifted up, shrugging out of it and tossing it to the floor.

"I never know what's going to happen next with you," he said, sucking in a breath as she undid his belt. She undid the button, slid down the zipper, but didn't release him. He watched the battle playing out behind her eyes as her hands slid up his body.

She moved toward him slowly, her eyes locked on his. Her long brown hair teased his skin as she made her way to him, darkening the room further as her face hovered inches from him. "Could you stop now?" her low voice taunted.

"Hannah," he threatened as her mouth came even closer, the heat from her breath wetting his lips.

"What about now?" She licked her lips, her tongue coming so close to his lips he felt her, but she didn't touch him.

"Anything you want," he ground out, forcing himself to be still. He wanted to touch her, but even more he wanted to find out just how she wanted to play.

She licked her lips again, the tip of her tongue caressing his bottom lip. As she retreated he followed her, maintaining the contact until she jerked away.

He lay back down in an invitation for her to continue her delicious tormenting. Again he watched her wage some internal battle. She was an amazing sight. The lace barely stretching over her heaving breasts, the dusty rose-colored nipples straining at the textured fabric, the flare of her hips as she sat atop him. The kind of beautiful that made a man ache to lose himself in her. Mason unclenched his fisted hands and let his fingers wrap around her hips. He wouldn't press her, he just needed more contact.

Her grin was wicked this time as she leaned down. She kissed him so gently he felt her smile. He captured her lips with his own, deepening the kiss. As she gave in he traced his fingers up her back, pulling down the straps to bare her shoulders. She pulled back slightly, looking at him accusingly. "Are you looking for something?"

He planted an open-mouthed kiss on her bare shoulder in response.

"I thought my outfit inspired you," she said, sitting up, pulling the straps to her shoulders.

"It inspires me to want more." He walked his fingers up her bent knees, up her thighs, under the hem of her chemise.

"More of me?" she asked breathily.

Mason nodded, and reminded himself he'd promised to stop if she asked. He had to stay in control of his body. Though from her position she must know how out of control the situation was becoming.

"How much more?" she asked, lifting the hem over his fingers to the flare of her hip. His hands chased the edge as she inched it up ever so slowly. She pulled past the matching lace thong, leaving Mason to wonder just how far Hannah took her bikini wax. "This much?" she asked, stopping just above her navel.

"More," he said, recognizing the pleading tone in his voice. She so had him. And he was enjoying every second of it.

She lifted the material slowly over her stomach, her ribcage, finishing the motion with a flourish as she whipped the chemise off her breasts and over her head. Her nipples looked as happy to be free of their lace prison as he was happy to see them. "Could you stop now, Mason?" she asked, rubbing her hands across the muscles of his shoulders as she leaned down until her nipples grazed his chest.

He bit his lip as he nodded, meeting her challenge. Just how far would she take this?

Lowering herself further, she kissed him. He deepened the kiss, savoring every nuance of her pliant mouth. As she gave into the kiss she felt her breasts pressing against his bare chest. He wasn't sure if she was testing him, but he opted to fail as he skimmed his hands from her hips up her body to the swell of her breasts. He swallowed her gasp as his fingers slowly traced the outer edge of her breasts. As she pulled back he stayed with her until he had her in the palms of his hands. He squeezed gently, passing his thumbs over her hardened buds.

"You like them," she said, pressing herself into his hands. "Could you stop without having tasted them?"

He froze, unsure. Could he really?

"I don't want you to," she whispered, leaning down and allowing him access with his mouth.

He fulfilled her request immediately, rolling her nipple on his tongue, before bringing it into his mouth with one long, hard pull. She moaned and her hand hit the pillow beside his head. Her hips lifted off his, relieving him of the torturous pressure.

He reveled in his new power, noting how her head was thrown back as he shifted his concentration to her other breast. One hand plucked the nipple he had just pleasured while the other hand skimmed her back, sliding her panties down her thighs. Reaching the front, he tugged them to her bent knees. He probably should worry about his own over-abundance of clothing, but he just had to know how wet she was.

His fingers skimmed across her trimmed landing strip and

into her hot folds. He was amazed by how slick she was, how ready. Primed. As if all he would have to do was curl his finger inside her and press her clit with his thumb...

She exploded, pressing back against his hand as the spasms rocked her and her knees gave out. He prolonged it for as long as he could, matching the contractions with the pulsing of his finger.

As they rolled onto their sides he used his free hand to brush the hair from her face, watching as her breathing returned to normal. Her eyelids fluttered open slowly. "Could you stop now?" she asked hoarsely. He stilled his hand and pulled it from between them. She laughed huskily and caught his wrist. "Only because you cheated."

"I didn't know the rules," he said, relieved they were still playing her game.

The musky scent of her pleasure filled his lungs, igniting a craving he'd had since he saw her in the robe. He bent toward her, tasting her collarbone and the well between her breasts. He went further, circling her belly button with his tongue. As he dipped lower she stilled him. "It's your turn."

"No, I cheated." He looked up at her, watching her eyes as he parted her thighs. "I lose a turn. You get to go again."

She grinned wickedly, propping herself up on her elbows. "Really, you don't have to. I don't think I can anyway."

"You think you can stop now?" he taunted, reaching his arms beneath her legs. She gasped as his fingers parted her, exposing her to him. He breathed her in, letting the warm air from his mouth tickle her body. As her hips began to lurch out of his hand he knew she could take another turn.

He tasted her slowly, flattening his tongue against her opening and sliding to the tip of her. He slid his tongue up one side and down the other, taunting her bud with each pass. He savored her smooth nuances, testing for what she liked best, and found the rhythm in her breathing. Sliding a finger inside, he felt her muscles begin to spasm. He felt the comforter rise beside them as she tore at it with clenched fists. He swirled around her clit, timing the motion with his finger, her choppy breaths. As he sucked it into his mouth her back arched into him and her muscles contracted around his finger. This time he didn't draw it out, simply withdrew and kissed his way up her body. He could wait, but not much longer. He paused, enjoying her breasts while he waited for her to come back to earth.

As her fingers massaged his scalp he heard her sweet voice, now raspy. "After that performance you can pretty much do anything you want to me."

He raised his head and looked into her eyes. "Anything I want?"

"I'm completely entranced with you right now." She grinned, running her fingertips up and down the contours of his well-muscled chest and rippled abs. Her voice purred, "Anything."

Shucking his socks, pants, and boxers, he lay back on the bed beside her and grinned. He knew exactly what he wanted. "I want to watch you come again."

Perhaps he hadn't heard her. She'd just offered herself up as his love slave and he wanted her to go again. As if she could. Twice in one night was already a personal best. But she was willing to do whatever got him off. It was only fair. Though a tour of what he'd had hidden in his pants would greatly improve her motivation.

She had to regain some control here. She'd been doing so well in the beginning, but somewhere along the way she'd lost her edge and given into the sensation. The man's tongue was positively lethal. Her eyes danced across his body, making her wish she hadn't turned off the lights. She wanted to see him, to feel him, taste him. It wasn't what he'd said he wanted but surely he wouldn't complain.

"I love it when you do that," he groaned, pulling her on top of him. "I just want to crawl inside your head and see all of the things you're thinking of doing to me."

The way his need throbbed between their bodies reminded her she needed to dig out the condoms stashed in her drawer; that way they'd both get what they wanted.

She sucked in air and willed the oxygen up to her brain. Her body was wound tight as a spring, not allowing her any thoughts but how to find release again.

Lifting herself up and relieving the pressure, she leaned forward and slid the nightstand drawer open. She fumbled around past her now irrelevant vibrator, finding the box in the back. She tried to open the cardboard carton with her fingers, but in frustration went at it with her teeth.

"A new box? Hannah, did you plan this?" he taunted her.

Finally removing a packet, she ripped it open. "Just be grateful one of us was prepared," she hissed, moving down his body for a better angle. She greedily grasped him and he jerked in her hand. A wicked laugh erupted from her throat as she felt his length, his girth. She was going to enjoy this so much.

Placing the condom over the swollen head, she bent down to roll the condom on with her mouth. His hands in her hair stopped the motion.

"Hannah, I'm so close," Mason ground out between clenched teeth. "If you do that, I swear, I'll come right away."

"You are?" she purred, wrapping her finger and thumb around the base of him and squeezing. She was relieved to have a little power back. He would wait for her; she'd make sure of that. "Better?" she teased, releasing him.

He moaned and fell back against the mattress.

"I thought you wanted to watch me," she taunted, tickling

his hips with the ends of her hair. She took the condom off the end of him, sucking him into her mouth with one long pull. His taste was tangy but not bitter. She'd definitely have to sample more of that later. She repeated the condom routine, and this time he managed to let her put it on.

"Mason," she whispered, looming over his body, drunk in her regained power. "Open your eyes."

She licked at his lips as his eyes slowly opened. "You're trying to kill me, aren't you?"

"Could you stop now?" she taunted, knowing he was just an inch from entering her.

"Hannah," he warned, his hands finding their way to her hips.

She reached between them, rubbing the tip of him against her wetness. "Could you?"

"Could you?" he threatened, locking her in his gaze. Shaking her head, she sank down slowly, filling herself with him as his eyes fluttered closed.

She froze. "Open your eyes or I'll stop."

His eyelids flew open at the threat. "Liar," he whispered, pulling her down completely.

She gasped at the stretching fullness. With her hands on his shoulders, she gave herself a moment to relish the sensation. When she couldn't stand it any more she began to rock her hips, not breaking eye contact.

"I want to watch you too," she panted, the pressure magically beginning to build yet again.

His hands drifted from her hips, one hand rising to knead her breast, pull her hard nipple. The thumb of the other hand was pressing between them where they joined.

"Mason, please. I want to wait for you," she heard herself beg him. And she didn't even care.

"You go and I won't be able to stop." His eyes told her it

was the truth. He was right there with her. She closed her eyes
and arched her back, soaking up every sensation his body was
pouring into her. She rode the sensation as the world narrowed and darkened, then exploded into a thousand colors
behind her eyelids. She heard screaming from somewhere.
Hers, his, she couldn't quite make out. Her body kept reminding her to breathe, as if she were drowning. At some point
the blankets covered them as they nestled together and as she
drifted off to dream she heard him whisper, "I knew it. I
knew from the way you kissed we'd be this way."

CHAPTER SIX

MASON heard her moving around in the kitchen. How was Hannah functioning when every muscle in his body was screaming? He rolled, opening one eye to read the display. Nine-fifteen. Late, but not too late considering he'd woken her up at least once last night for another round. Maybe it was twice. With Hannah it was hard to tell when he was dreaming.

Throwing off the blankets, he sat up and slowly stretched, allowing his body to adjust to the new day. And work out the kinks from the most amazing night of his life. He hadn't just dreamed her up. She was real, and, if he heard right, cussing in the kitchen.

He thought about going out there naked as he would at home, but stepped into his knit boxers instead. He couldn't tell just what she was doing out there.

He found her digging through the refrigerator in search of something interesting. From the looks of the carnage in the paper bag beside her she wasn't having much luck. "Need some help?" he asked, leaning over the door. She was in a different robe, a steely-blue flannel. Not a good sign.

She looked up at him with a forced grin. "I'm sorry if I woke you."

He retreated to the counter, not sure what to expect from

her cool demeanor. Closing the refrigerator, she walked the bag to the door, then circled back into the kitchen. She stood in front of the sink, crossed her arms across her chest and blew out a long breath.

He stared hard at her, willing her to meet his gaze. When she did he saw it: morning-after remorse. It kicked him in the gut. He stepped to her slowly and wrapped his arms around her stiff body.

"I know what you must think of me," she whispered, "after that little stunt I pulled last night. I wish you knew me better because I'm not really like that."

"Like what?" he asked, pulling back to look at her. He lifted her chin from where she had buried her face in his chest. "Sexy, confident and daring?"

"You are really being nice about this." She wriggled free, turned and grabbed a mug from the cupboard.

"I'll warn you," he said, clearing his throat. "If you tell me you regret it, it just might kill me."

Her eyes met his again. He saw her trying to decide if he meant it. "I've never been with somebody so soon. I'm a little turned around this morning."

Mason nodded, hoping to assuage her embarrassment. "Maybe if you eat something you'll feel better. I know I'm starving."

Hannah smiled back. "Me too, that's what prompted my little cleaning episode. I was looking for something to eat, but since I usually just grab something while I'm out, there was nothing but ancient take-out containers in my fridge."

He grinned, finally finding the edge he was looking for. "Lucky for you I can cook, and I only live upstairs. These are some fabulous selling points for keeping me around." He took her hand and pulled her to the door.

"You want me to walk upstairs dressed, or rather undressed, like this?"

His gaze traveled up and down the robe. It covered her more completely than anything he'd seen yesterday. But her nipples tented the soft fabric, reminding him she wore nothing beneath it. "I do, I really do."

No one caught them wandering the halls in their underwear, Hannah thought in relief as they snuck down the hall to Mason's apartment. Thank goodness for small favors. If there was a kinky neighbor, cruising around in her bathrobe was asking for trouble. But she hadn't been able to resist as Mason had dropped her keys in her bathrobe pocket and pulled her out the door.

She didn't seem to be able to resist Mason at all, come to think of it. The man had come over to try and accommodate her frenzied work schedule and she'd jumped him as soon as she'd had the chance. She hadn't been shy about it either. Teasing and taunting and tempting. What must he think of her?

Neither of the other men she'd been involved with would have ever played along with her little game. Or given her five orgasms before sunrise. Her body still hummed from the experience. She didn't like the power that gave him. Now that Mason knew just how much she liked sex, he could use it to manipulate her.

And that gave him even more of a hold on her. She swallowed hard as Mason finally opened the door to his apartment. He probably thought she was a closet dominatrix, immediately tumbling into bed with any man who looked her way. He might expect her to be like last night every time. She used to be shy, but Mason had fueled a fire she always tried to hide.

As Mason shut the door behind her Hannah surveyed his apartment. It seemed larger than hers, though the square footage was identical. Instead of having a hallway and two bedrooms, his had a larger living area with open doors leading to the bedroom and bath. Two black leather sofas cornered to face an entertainment center on the opposite wall. The coffee table between them was piled with magazines.

"You can have a seat, or you can help me in the kitchen," Mason said, releasing her hand and walking into a kitchen identical to her own. Except Mason obviously used more than just the microwave. Stainless-steel pots and pans hung from a pot rack over the sink. A bowl of fruit sat on top of a large wooden cutting board covering the part of the counter she and Kate used to sort the mail. As he opened the fridge she noticed it was full. Her mouth watered at the sight of milk and orange juice and bread and butter. A person could actually live here.

"What's your pleasure?" he asked without removing his head from the fridge. "Omelets, French toast, waffles, pancakes?"

Was this an apartment or a restaurant? "You'll make me waffles?"

Mason turned, lifting her gaze with his own. "Anything you want."

"My dad used to make us waffles on Sunday mornings to get us to go with Mom to church," she said, stepping into the kitchen.

"Waffles it is." He began opening containers and dumping powders into a bowl without using anything but his hands to measure.

"Do you have peanut butter?" she asked hesitantly. He spun, magically producing a jar of creamy and a jar of chunky and placing them on the counter before her. "Did you plan this?" She laughed, cocking her hip against the counter.

"I wish I'd thought of it," he said with a shrug. "My mom always spoiled us with a stocked kitchen. I got a little too used to it, I guess."

"How many of you are there?" It stung to realize how little she knew about a man she'd shared so much of herself with.

He turned and smiled, that single dimple melting her resolve to stay cool. "There's just one of me. But there are five McNally boys."

Five of them? "God bless your mother."

"You don't know the half of it," he said as Hannah watched his hands. Strong, skillful, purposeful hands that could pleasure, protect, and provide. "She'll never admit it, but she always wanted a girl. When my brother Ryan had Riana two years ago, my mother nearly came out of her skin she was so excited. She even retired when Ryan's wife went back to work, just to have Riana to herself every day."

Hannah did not want to discuss babies with Mason. Things were on fast-forward with them already. Back to safer subjects. "Your mother taught you to cook?"

Mason nodded. "I think she felt guilty about introducing so much testosterone into the world, so she made sure we all cook, make the bed, and iron our own shirts. She's almost militant about it."

She watched him moving effortlessly about the small space. It was almost like dancing, the way he coordinated his movements. "My sister has a firehouse cookbook she swears by. Do you have to cook a lot at work?"

"Not really, we all take turns. Cooking here is easy. At work it's harder because you have to be able to stop at any point. It's frustrating." His eyes met hers, realizing the connection to last night. "Challenging," he corrected himself. "I love a good challenge."

She hadn't been much of a challenge last night the way she'd dragged him to her bedroom.

But Mason relaxed her, made her feel safe and comfortable with just a glance. He seemed to be following through on his promise that it wouldn't be just one night. Maybe for the next six weeks she'd let her inhibitions go and be the daring sex kitten she'd been last night.

She heard a spoon drop and looked up to find Mason right in front of her.

"I love it when you do that." He leaned down and slowly kissed her neck. She could smell sex and chocolate and—was that banana?

"I don't even know when I'm doing it." She stilled his hands as they reached for the belt of her bathrobe. "I thought you were going to make me a waffle."

"Right." He pulled away with a slow grin and returned to his task. She smiled at the tent in the front of his boxers. "What time do you have to be at work today?"

She technically wasn't scheduled to start until two, but she was always in by eleven in the morning on the nights she closed. The clock on his microwave showed it was past nine. No time for anything but breakfast and a shower, alone, if she wanted to get there by eleven. "Not until two." The store wouldn't fall apart without her for a few hours. She might even be more productive tonight with a spring in her step.

Mason turned, arching an eyebrow. "What time are you off?"

Was he trying to keep tabs on her or just figuring out how long until he got laid again? "I close, so I'll be done around eleven, but I work at five in the morning tomorrow. I need to get some sleep tonight." *Alone. To think about just what I've gotten myself into here.*

"I have to be in Saturday by seven. When are you off Sunday?"

"The store closes at eight. Do you want me to print you out a copy of my schedule?" she teased.

He didn't catch the joke. "I can't wait until Thursday," he

said, setting glasses of orange juice on his kitchen table. He unloaded more things from the cupboards and refrigerator. Maple syrup, butter, whipped cream.

Whipped cream? Was he tempting her with sides the way she'd teased him last night? Seeing that, she wasn't planning on waiting until breakfast was over.

Hannah sat in one of the two chairs at the small table and watched as Mason moved about the kitchen in his underwear. It was the most intimately domestic moment she'd ever shared with a man. How did this happen so fast?

Just as quickly Mason slipped her waffle in front of her and slid into the chair across from her. Hannah's stomach growled. She focused on fueling her body. She'd need energy for all she was imagining.

She slathered chunky peanut butter across the steaming waffle, just as she used to when she was a kid. Crunchy peanut butter and creamy melting chocolate chips, sweet banana and crispy waffle exploded in her mouth and an involuntary moan escaped her throat.

Mason laughed, rubbing his foot against her bare calf as he dug into his own waffle. "I definitely don't get that reaction at work."

Hannah held herself in check, forcing herself to eat slowly and not embarrass herself again. For a girl used to getting most of her sustenance from the vending machine in the break room at work, this was a rare piece of heaven.

"I can make you another one," Mason offered. Looking up, Hannah noticed he was only half finished with his. And she'd been forcing herself to go slow.

She shook her head. "Thanks for making breakfast. It was really nice of you."

"Anytime, anywhere, anything," he said as he finished his plate.

Hannah felt herself losing her nerve. It was all good and well to fantasize about seducing the man, but reality was different. He'd made it so easy for her last night. Or she'd been easy. Maybe he was just being nice now so she'd sleep with him again. Was he manipulating her? "That's quite a line. Do you use it often?"

"It's not a line, Hannah." He shook his head and rose from the table, taking their plates to the sink. "I never pegged you for insecure."

Hannah's stomach sank. It was happening already. He'd start using how much she enjoyed sex against her, withdrawing if she criticized or argued. "I'm going to go get ready for work."

He spun around, one hand clutching chocolate syrup, the other whipped cream. The man looked like an advertisement for sin. "Already? Give me a second and I'll go with you."

So he could show how sensitive he was—and get back into her bed. "I can make it down a flight of stairs by myself, Mason."

Hannah made her way to the door, not realizing his bare feet followed silently behind her. As she opened the front door his hand came down on it, slamming it closed. "You're not leaving."

She turned, pinned between his body and the door. Mason knew how it might look. How she might feel. But something was going on in her head that didn't bode well for him, for them, and he wasn't about to let her walk away.

He swallowed hard, watched as her breath hitched, her breasts rising and falling rapidly between them. Behind her eyes he watched the battle, for the first time not loving the fire he saw there.

"Something has been wrong since you woke up and you're not going anywhere until we fix it."

She stopped breathing, and he held his breath too. He'd pushed her too far, too fast last night. He'd known it as it had been happening, but he hadn't been able to help himself. She was just so beautiful. He moved one hand down to brush her soft cheek and she looked up at him with wide eyes, innocent eyes.

He just needed to make her feel safe with him, then she'd relax. A soft, gentle good-morning kiss, as he should have given her earlier, would do the trick. As he leaned in she ducked under his arm and away from the door.

"Is this how it usually works for you?" Hannah spat at him. "You make breakfast for a woman so she'll sleep with you again?"

He shouldn't have tried for the kiss. "Is this how you usually handle the morning after?" he replied, mimicking her tone. "I made breakfast because we were hungry, no ulterior motive."

"Right," she sneered. "Like last night you *just* stopped by to compare schedules."

Where in the world was all of this coming from? "You want to tell me what this is about? Because I really don't think it has anything to do with me."

"Derek's the shrink, not you," she said, plopping down on his couch. The crinkle of leather filled the silence as she tucked her feet beneath her, carefully wrapping her robe around her naked body.

Mason stepped slowly to the foot of the coffee table. He was sure she'd bolt if he tried to sit down. "What's wrong?" he asked, ignoring her barb about his brother. Wanting to wrap his hands around the neck of whoever had hurt her bad enough to make her this fearful, this suspicious.

"I don't know you," she said quietly, picking at her finger-nails. "I don't know you, and I had sex with you, and I'm a little freaked out about it, okay?"

His head cocked to the side as he studied her. "That's what last night felt like to you? Like strangers having sex?" he asked, knowing the answer. Her eyes told him it felt like an entirely different emotion, and that was what had her running scared.

She hugged her knees tighter and looked up at him. "How many women have you been with, Mason?"

A woman could never be satisfied with any answer to that question. "I'm thirty-two, Hannah. I'm hardly a virgin."

She looked away and huffed, "Yeah, I could tell."

Now, that was a cheap shot. "Hannah, knock it off. I'm trying to be understanding here and you're being rude." Where was his sweet, soft Hannah, and how was he supposed to get rid of this suspicious, aggressive, bitchy twin?

"And calling me insecure was *so* nice," she sneered, laying her head against her knees.

His stomach clenched with the realization he'd hurt her with those words. She looked so small, curled on his couch, trying to get a grip on what she was feeling.

"I'm sorry if it hurt you. It was an observation, not a dig." He felt the pain and fear radiating from her, warning him to tread carefully instead of react to her barbs. "You're so confident about everything. I never expected you to be intimidated by anything."

She took in two deep breaths, seeming to prepare herself for something. "You are only the third man I've ever been with, Mason." Her voice was barely more than a whisper. "And I haven't been with anyone in a year and a half. My hormones overruled my head last night. You probably think I do that kind of act all the time, but I never have. And I doubt I'll ever be able to pull it off again."

"I figured," he said, stepping slowly toward her.

"What? How?" she asked, her eyes wide.

"Your reaction this morning was a dead giveaway, but I knew last night." Kneeling beside her, he rubbed his fingers across the toes peeking from below her robe. "You turned off all the lights and sometimes your hands were shaking."

She closed her eyes and pressed her lips together until they were white. "And I thought I was embarrassed before."

"Hannah, you have nothing to be embarrassed about. You're every man's fantasy. I'm sorry, I shouldn't have pushed it last night."

"I wanted it more than you did," she admitted, relaxing her grip on her knees.

"I don't think that's humanly possible." Mason smiled up at her.

She let out a long, sad sigh. "I just wish we knew each other better. I don't even know your middle name."

"What?" He laughed.

"It's a girl thing. You want to know about the man you're sleeping with, even his middle name."

"So if you knew more about me you'd feel better about last night?" As she nodded he began to have some hope his horniness last night hadn't ruined everything. "Okay, twenty questions. The only rule is you can't ask me anything you won't answer yourself."

"Twenty questions?"

He felt as skeptical as she sounded, but it was all that came to mind. "Yes, and we can start with middle names. Mine's Mason; what's yours?"

"What?"

"Mason is my middle name."

"What's your first name, then?"

"You have to play by the rules, Hannah," he said, climbing onto the couch next to her. "You answer my question, then you get to ask one of your own."

"Fine, but you better not laugh. It's Faye. Now what is your first name?" She was smiling.

"Hannah Faye. I like it. But you can't laugh either. It was my grandfather's name and he died when my mom was pregnant so I got stuck with it." He paused for effect, then whispered, "Francis."

He smiled as she winced. "It doesn't fit you at all."

"That's because it's not my name; it was his. Where did yours come from?"

"Are you sure you want to use one of your questions?" Her grin was back in full as she turned to face him on the couch, tucking her legs beneath her. "I didn't ask for that little history lesson, so it doesn't count toward mine."

He didn't know whether to shake his head or nod. "Are you always going to beat me at my own game?"

"Plan on it."

Tension was evaporating off her body as they talked. Maybe she hadn't been a complete idiot to sleep with this man. In way over her head, sure, but just maybe it wasn't a mistake. Once she stopped assuming the worst and forced herself to look beyond his made-for-sin exterior, he was actually very sweet.

Mason could have tossed her aside like yesterday's trash, both for her vamp imitation last night and her attack of conscience this morning. But he had stayed the course, made her a delicious breakfast and agreed to play twenty questions just to make her feel better. With that and his stellar performance in bed last night, a girl needed to be careful or she'd find herself in way too deep.

"My turn," Mason said, extending their game that should've ended fifteen questions ago. "Have you ever been engaged?"

"Why is it all of your questions are about relationships and mine are about personal history?"

"Relationships are personal history." He somehow made a shrug seem confident. "You want me to go first?"

She didn't want to know about the women he'd been with before, but nodded anyway.

"Never. Never even an 'I love you'."

Hannah had only heard 'I love you' from a man who clearly hadn't, a jerk who'd used the phrase just to get her to sleep with him. She swallowed hard, hoping that wasn't what was happening now. She wanted more from Mason, more than casual, more than sexual blackmail.

She'd been so touched when Marty had confessed his love. She hadn't loved him, but she'd always hoped someone would be as devoted to her as he'd seemed. Too bad the snake was incapable of truth.

"Where did you just go?" Mason asked, his fingers lazily dancing across her arm.

"I've never been engaged either," she said with a quick sigh and what she hoped was a carefree smile. It wasn't a lie. When Dalton had decided it was time to get married, she'd insisted they sleep together first. It had been bland and boring, and yet still she'd clung to it for a while, hoping it would get better. Until he'd started using her sex drive against her, withholding sex unless she did what he wanted, making her feel lewd and dirty.

When she'd ended it and started dating, her parents had been furious. "Good girls don't spread themselves around, Hannah." As if she'd been able to bring herself to do more than just kiss. She'd used those kisses as a barometer. If she'd felt nothing, there had been no need to take it further anyway.

If only she'd kept it that way. There had been nothing when Marty had kissed her either; the sex only marginally better. But she'd stuck with it because of the way he'd pursued her. He'd supported every career move, even new store openings that had taken her out of state for months at a time. How convenient for him.

"And my second question? Where did you go just now?"

"It's not your turn." Hannah scrambled for a question good enough to distract him. "Where was your first kiss?"

"Hannah, come on, what was that about?" His eyes pinned her to the couch, his fingers wrapped around her wrist.

"You don't like my question? I thought you wanted to talk about relationships." She didn't want him to know how easily she'd been fooled, how easily he could take advantage of her.

"Fine. Seventh grade, Denise London, spin the bottle, she bit me."

"She bit you?" Hannah stifled a giggle.

"Your turn," he said without smiling, blinking, or releasing his grip.

She squirmed beneath the pressure. "It was my sophomore year, Nathan Brady, touchdown at the football game Friday night. My sister told my folks and I was grounded for two weeks."

"Why?"

"I was only fifteen. We weren't allowed to date until we were sixteen. Nice girls don't kiss boys they aren't dating, so I was busted by default."

"That's harsh. Now it's my turn."

"You just had your turn. You asked me why."

Mason pulled on her wrist, yanking her forward to within an inch of him. "Come on. I want to know."

His eyes were so intent they had a steely quality. He wasn't going to let it go, and she was not going there. "I need to shower and get ready for work."

"When the game is over."

"Mason. It was over twenty questions ago." She tried to pull away but he held firm. "Let it go or I shower alone."

"What?" he asked, releasing her immediately.

"You do have a shower, don't you?" Hannah asked, standing up, willing herself not to shake as she extended a hand to him. She could do this. If Mason liked sex half as much as she did she'd use it against him too. He'd forget all about her little lapse, and she'd forget everything for a moment.

Hannah watched Mason's eyes as he studied her, weighing her proposition. She wondered if that was what her eyes did that he liked so much. She wasn't sure she liked it. It looked as if he was about to say no.

Without dropping her gaze or taking her hand, Mason rose from the couch, gave her a dastardly grin, and dropped his boxers.

She'd thought he was magnificent last night, but some things were even better in the light. As he stood there in all his glory she couldn't help but lick her lips. Her hand instinctively went to the source of her pleasure, but he caught her wrist.

His voice vibrated through her. "Your turn."

He released her hand and she met his dare, dropping her robe to the floor.

She watched his gaze center on the white cotton panties she'd slipped on this morning. "I love the way you tease me." He dropped his shoulder and stepped toward her, picking her up and throwing her over his shoulder.

"Mason!" She giggled, bouncing against his back as he carried her to the bathroom.

CHAPTER SEVEN

"HANNAH? Are you in there?"

Hannah froze midstep. Behind her on the staircase, Mason wrapped his arm around her waist to keep from knocking her down.

"Do you know him?" he whispered in her ear, his wet hair cold against her temple.

She nodded, not wanting to speak. Wanting nothing more than to sink into the floor right now.

"Who?" Mason asked without moving.

"It's my brother-in-law. Maybe he'll go away." She swallowed hard, listening for retreating footsteps. Instead she jumped, hearing her phone ringing inside her apartment.

"It must be important," Mason whispered.

"He's going to know what we were doing." She hated the whining sound in her voice.

"We're adults, Hannah." She heard his jaw grinding as he whispered in her ear. "But I'll go back upstairs if you want."

That might spare her a few lectures, since Troy knew that as of just a week ago she wasn't seeing anyone. She turned and ran her hands up the fire-department sweatshirt he'd put on after the most athletic shower of her life. "That's sweet of you to offer, but it still wouldn't explain my wet hair and bathrobe."

"Or lack of panties," he whispered naughtily in her ear.

She kissed him gently, savoring the different feel of his upper lip since he'd shaved. "Fast forward," she whispered to herself as she turned, took Mason's hand and made her way to her own front door. She'd already slept with him; maybe it wasn't too early to start introducing him to the family.

"Is there a problem, Troy?" Hannah asked, fishing her key from the pocket of her robe.

Troy stared open-mouthed at them. Quickly Hannah opened the door and ushered both men inside. She'd given her neighbors enough to talk about already.

Closing the door behind her, she made introductions. "Troy, I don't mean to be rude, but what are you doing here?"

"Molly's worried about you. You haven't returned her calls. She wanted to come herself, but I told her I'd check in."

It had only been three days since she'd last talked to Molly. She hadn't wanted the third degree about her date with Mason. She barely knew what was going on and she didn't care to explain it to anyone else.

"Molly's a worrier. I'm fine." Hannah wished Troy would stop looking at Mason as if he'd done something wrong. Troy was two years younger than her; she didn't need him pulling the "protective older brother" act.

"Why is…? Where were…?" Troy's hands were flying about.

"I live upstairs," Mason stated, as if it would answer anything.

Apparently it did because Troy started to nod furiously. "Hannah, can I talk to you for a second, privately?"

"No." Hannah walked to the door and opened it. No way was she giving Troy an opportunity to lecture her. "Tell Molly I'll call her tomorrow."

Troy's eyes narrowed as he stalked toward the door, kicking a red envelope straight into Hannah's foot.

She yelped and picked it up, her mouth going dry as she realized it wasn't addressed.

Time slowed as Mason crossed the room and removed it from her hand, opening it to reveal a picture of a red velvet bra and panty set, trimmed in white fur like so many of the Santa sets she'd seen in the stores. Mason shoved the card back in the envelope with a curse.

"You okay?" he asked, wrapping his arm around her.

Hannah squared her shoulders and took a deep breath. "It could be nothing, Mason." Probably a neighbor annoyed by all the noise they'd made last night.

"I still don't like it," he said as she shrugged him off.

"What?" Troy demanded from the doorway.

"A kinky neighbor has slipped cards under my door a couple of times," Hannah said, watching Troy's eyes focus on Mason. "Not him." She dismissed the notion with a wave of her hand.

"Hannah, I need to talk to you, alone," Troy insisted, coming back over and grabbing her arm.

"Don't touch her," Mason said with an edge to his voice Hannah hadn't heard before.

She shook off Troy's grasp and stepped between the men. "I need to get ready for work."

"When did you get the other cards?" Troy asked, unmoved.

"There was just one, Wednesday some time. It's probably nothing."

"Wasn't Wednesday the night you went out with him?" Troy demanded, his face reddening.

"Troy, I'm not in the mood." She wanted the last ten minutes to be erased from her life forever.

"Hannah, what are you thinking?" he said, shaking his head. "Use your brain. You can't be this stupid again."

"Okay, that's enough," Mason said, stepping out from behind Hannah. "You want to talk to her, that's one thing, but you don't insult her in her own home. I don't care if you are family."

Hannah threw her hands up in the air and stepped out from between the two men towering over her. "You two feel free to take this outside. I'm going to go get dressed."

Hannah tried to listen as she went through the motions of getting ready for work. She was relieved she didn't hear anything breaking. But she didn't hear the yelling she was expecting either.

Hannah was glad for the pinstriped black suit and heels. They made her feel much more authoritative and in control than she'd been barefoot and naked beneath her bathrobe. She was sure the cards were nothing, but she'd call the building manager anyway and see if he had any ideas. And it might give Mason an incentive to start sleeping over.

As Hannah emerged from the hallway she was disappointed to find Troy alone in the apartment. "Where's Mason?" she asked, not bothering to hide her hurt that he'd leave without saying goodbye.

"Why are you so sure it's not him?" Troy asked from his perch on the sofa. "He could be trying to scare you so he could play the hero."

That one was easy. "Each time a card's shown up, he's been with me."

"Maybe he's having someone else deliver them."

Hannah saw where he was going with this and cut him off. "Troy, this is not your problem."

"If it wasn't him… When was the last time you heard from Marty?"

"What? Why?" Hannah asked, her stomach sinking.

"He was really angry when I went to his wife. Then again,

Mason mentioned some guy from work was eyeing you. Could it be him?"

"Where is Mason?" she asked again, not wanting to create a list of suspects for a crime that consisted of spending too much time at Hallmark.

As if on cue, Mason appeared in the doorway with a box. He began pressing some kind of tape to her door frame.

"What are you doing?" she asked as he continued to play with her doorway as if she'd given him permission.

"Making sure that little chicken shit doesn't slide anything through the door anymore." Mason replied without looking at her, so her annoyed expression didn't register.

"With what?" Troy asked, crossing to the doorway. The two men were oblivious to her presence, focused on solving the problem, not on her.

"I'm fireproofing it." Mason's eyes didn't move from his task. "When the door is closed it will seal so tight an envelope won't fit through."

"I always thought you were crazy," Mason said to the long, jean-clad legs sticking out from beneath the black GTO. The car had been in the garage for at least fifteen years and he'd never even heard the engine run.

"You all did at one point," Mac McNally said, sliding out from beneath the car. His hands and shirt were clean, as if he was lying beneath the car for fun. "Why am I crazy today?"

"I don't think you are. I think you must be a genius."

"Flattery will get you nowhere with me, kid. You still have to help me move the table out before you leave. Grab me a beer, will you?" Mac got up slowly and grabbed a rag and canister of wax off his workbench.

Mason carefully maneuvered the cans from the too-full fridge. With just under two weeks until Thanksgiving the main fridge in the McNally garage had been taken over for the festivities. It gave Mason a little pang of regret that he'd miss so much of it.

Mason handed the can to his father and popped open his own. "I need some advice."

"From me? You never listen to me. This has got to be good," Mac said with a chuckle. "I'd call your mom in, but she's taken Riana to the mall for portraits, again."

"No, for this I actually need you. How did you get Mom to marry you after just three days without freaking her out?" He took a long slow drink, shoring up his courage before meeting his father's gaze.

Mac gave a shrug, then leveled his gaze at his middle son. "Your mother doesn't scare easy. Is she Catholic?"

Mason rolled his eyes. "Come on, did Mom ask you that?"

"With a name like McNally she didn't have to. What's her last name?"

Thank God she'd handed him her mail. "Daniels."

"No help there. You'll have to ask her," Mac said with a nod.

Mason shook his head. "That doesn't matter to me, Dad."

"It should." He punctuated his statement with a long drink.

"Really? When was the last time you went to Mass?"

"Your mother goes for me," Mac said, polishing an imaginary spot on the car. "How long have you known this girl?"

"I first met her a couple of weeks ago, but we had a misunderstanding." Mason didn't want to go into the particulars. His dad wouldn't be any happier he'd agreed to Derek's experiment than Hannah had been. "I found her again a few day ago."

Mac spun around, leaving the rag on the car. "Is this the girl Derek went out with?"

Derek and his big mouth. "They did not go out, Dad. They met for coffee so we could explain about the misunderstanding."

"That's not how Derek told the story. He said he was having coffee, minding his own business, and you waltzed in and kissed the girl all the way out the door."

Mason had to laugh at Derek's theatrics. He gave in and filled his father in on the facts of the story, from their first meeting to their first date. "I knew that first time I saw her, Dad, that's why I couldn't stand not knowing where she was. I always thought you and Mom were crazy to get married so quickly, but now I get it. You just know."

"We both knew, Mason," Mac said with a sympathetic smile. "It sounds like your girl isn't so sure. You could be wrong about this."

"I'm not." Mason shook his head emphatically. There was no doubt in his mind, not after last night. "I just don't want to spook her. Everything is moving a little fast for her and she hasn't figured out why yet."

"Then slow it down. There's no need to try and end the race if there's no finish line. If you're sure, bring her for Thanksgiving."

Mason nodded. He wasn't even off until seven-thirty on Thanksgiving. By the time he got out here most of the family would be drunk on tryptophan and champagne. And probably having one of their famous hands-free pie-eating contests. Not the best first impression for Hannah.

"There is something else I wanted to ask you about," Mason said, handing his father the two cards, explaining they'd been slipped under Hannah's door. Mac had seen everything in his thirty years on the police force, maybe he could give some insight into the problem.

Mac handed them back and looked Mason in the eye. "Unsigned cards are pretty benign; she's probably okay as long as it sticks to cards." He changed his expression. "Could she be doing it?"

"No. Why would she do that?" Mason asked with a laugh. The last card hadn't been there when they'd left and he hadn't taken his eyes off of her.

"Sometimes people invent things for attention, or to be saved."

"She's not. Her brother-in-law actually thinks I'm doing it. He was there when we got the card this morning, which is weird. He said he was checking in because her sister was worried, but I'd never just show up at Ryan and Tara's. I don't know. Derek's friends with him, but, still, it was strange timing."

"If you wanted to be a detective you should have joined the force like your brothers."

Mason shook his head at the argument he'd been having for the last ten years. The argument his youngest brother, Tyler, was currently embroiled in. So far only two of the five McNally boys had joined the force. Mac had always planned on a clean sweep. "Hannah thinks it's a neighbor because you need a code to get into the building."

"Where you also live, which is why the brother-in-law suspects you."

"Right, but he got in and he doesn't live there. Plus there's this guy she works with who was eyeing her."

"There's not a lot you can do with just a couple of cards, Mason. If there are any messages on them, have one of your brothers look into it."

He was not about to sit on his hands and wait for something to happen to her. This was the woman he'd been looking for his entire life. He wasn't going to let anything get in the way of that. Even her.

Hannah loved her job. From the moment she'd walked in the door until she turned the key to lock up she hadn't obsessed about Mason, or Troy, or the damn cards. There had been so much to get done before she spent the next few days leading the motivational seminars, she hadn't allowed herself a single self-indulgent thought.

She didn't have time for any now, either. She needed to get on the train, get home, and get some sleep. She had to unlock the same door in just six hours.

Hannah sighed as she fell in step behind a group of women who also took the train and checked her watch. Seven minutes until the train was due to arrive, forty-one until she made her station. She should have taken Mason up on his offer to drive her home, but she hadn't wanted to encourage this protective streak he was nurturing. She wasn't some damsel in distress. She could take care of herself.

Hannah surveyed the parking lot as they made their way across to the park-and-ride terminal. It was emptying quickly as her staff made their way home. She should get another car; it might save her some time. But taking the train was more economical. Gas, insurance and paying to park a car downtown was too expensive to be practical. She'd much rather save her money, just in case. She'd get some work done on the train anyway.

The click from her heels echoed in her ears as she tightened her coat around her. She looked up, checking to make sure all the parking lot lights were on. It just seemed so dark. She pulled the strap of her bag higher on her shoulder and quickened her pace to keep step with the group in front of her. Damn those cards—they were making her paranoid.

"Hannah."

She heard her name and froze, watching as the three women in front of her turned first to the voice and then to her. She knew who it was. Their faces watched for her reaction, as they always did.

The store might be closed, but she was still on the clock.

She schooled her expression and reached into her coat pocket for her keys, fingering the pepper spray on her keyring. He'd never tried to hurt her physically before, but he'd also never surprised her in a dark parking lot.

"Go ahead, ladies; I'll make the train," she said with a confident smile. She didn't want them to hear anything he might have to say. She worked hard to keep what there was of her private life separate from the gossip mill at work. She'd be fielding enough questions from this little stunt already.

Once the women were out of earshot she finally turned, noticing Marty was leaning against a late-model silver Jaguar. "New car?" she asked, trying to sound light, flippant, as if she hadn't broken out in a cold sweat.

"It's your fault." The words slurred and she noticed the bottle in his hand. Great, he was drunk. "She left me because of you." He raised his hand and pointed a finger at her. Or in her direction; he was obviously seeing double.

"Your girlfriend or your wife?" She couldn't help herself. As he stepped forward she realized it wasn't smart to provoke him, given his current state.

"Why did you have to open your fat mouth? That was so stupid, Hannah, so stupid." He stepped closer, steaming puffs of breath leaving his mouth with every word he spat her way. The stench of whiskey permeated the air, making her stomach lurch.

"Don't come any closer, Marty," Hannah said, her voice hoarse from the bile burning the back of her throat.

"Or what?" he asked with a sneer. "You'll scream? You wouldn't want someone from work to hear you, to know what a whore you are. Wouldn't want to tarnish your little career."

She wanted to go, to run, but she didn't want to turn her

back on him either. Or let him know he was scaring her. "Do you want me to call you a cab?"

"I'm fine." His fist slammed against the car, shattering the bottle he held.

Hannah's breath caught in her belly as she watched the glass splinter apart, thousands of pieces falling in slow motion. She heard each shard clink and ping as it hit the blacktop and glistened in the lamplight. Her fingers clasped the pepper spray, though she noticed it wasn't a match for broken glass. Why hadn't she just kept walking?

He raised the neck of the bottle he still held in his hand, a sinister laugh vibrating in the blackness as the shard of glass glistened with his blood. "See what you made me do? You always made me do crazy things, Hannah."

He must be really drunk. The slice in his hand didn't even bother him. Hannah looked around her. She could run. She was remarkably agile in heels, so running was an option. But running meant turning her back on a man with a weapon. "Marty, you come any closer and, I swear, I will scream." With one hand on her pepper spray she slowly reached the other into her bag, hoping to find her cell phone.

"It's been a long time, Hannah. I didn't know you'd be so jealous." He jerked his head toward her bag. "What are you trying to find in there?"

Jealous? He was really drunk. "My cell phone. I'm going to call you a cab. You can't drive with your hand sliced up."

His laugh sliced through her as he moved closer. She matched his step, backing away. "I bet I know what you're looking for. Don't worry; I have condoms in the car. I know you want me; that's why you ruined things with Lisa."

No, no, no. This was *not* happening. "I just gave Lisa the information I wish I'd had." Finding the phone, she finally let out a breath, flipping it open without taking it from the bag.

"The bitch told her, went right to my house and told her. When I got home she and the kids were gone. Mary says she believed her because of that stuff your brother-in-law showed her. She left because of you. Because you want us to be together."

She pulled the phone out, continuing to back away as he stepped closer. "It's your call, Marty. Stay back or I call the police instead of a cab."

His eyes ran over her once, twice, as he licked his lips. He raised his foot to step closer and her heart stopped. The crunch of tires on pavement startled them both and Marty raised his arm, shielding his eyes from the headlights blinding him from behind her.

She spun, taking in the boxy old Bronco and its driver as he jumped to the ground. "Get in the truck," he snapped at her.

She hadn't known she could get any more scared. Every muscle in her body, already on red alert, tensed further as she watched Mason step in front of Marty. The relief of escaping from Marty was overridden by her fear for Mason. Of Mason.

"In the truck, Hannah," Mason ordered without looking at her.

She walked obediently to the passenger side but didn't get in. She didn't take too well to orders, and she wasn't altogether sure just what was happening.

"You need to go, now," Mason growled. Marty tightened his grip on the broken bottle neck. Her stomach tensed in an all-new terror as Marty's gaze drifted from Mason to her with a lecherous smile.

"You want me to tell him how you like it?"

Her eyes closed as she heard the sound of falling, cracking, grunting. Words she didn't want to try to make out. She opened her eyes and watched as the bottle neck spun across the parking lot. Further and further away. She wanted to run right after it. And keep running until her life returned to normal.

She heard the siren before she saw the flashing lights illuminate the parking lot. Mason froze, his knee digging into Marty's back, his hand contorting the other man's arm behind him. She said a prayer; grateful she didn't have to learn exactly what Mason would have done to Marty.

In the distance Hannah saw her three employees huddled together watching the event unfold like a bad episode of reality television. They must have been watching all along, probably calling the police when they'd realized she was in over her head.

Two policemen leapt from their squad car, drawing their guns. Hannah squeezed her eyes tight against the image. When had this become her life?

"Mason?" a voice she didn't recognize asked.

"Hey, Ryan. I could use a little help here."

"His brother was the cop that showed up?" Kate asked, fluffing the chenille blanket covering them on the couch.

Hannah nodded and sipped her extra-strength tea, hoping there was enough caffeine in the world to get her through the day. She hadn't gotten back from the police station until almost two, when Ryan had driven her home.

Since she had to be dressed and ready for work in two hours, there was no point in trying to sleep. The only bright spot in her nightmare was that Kate had decided to come home after all. It was exactly what Hannah needed to feel safe.

"Did Mason even try to explain why he was there?"

"He said he wanted to make sure I was all right. He wanted to give me a ride home from the station and explain more, but I just couldn't listen to it." Hannah took another long draw of the hot tea, grateful for the burning sensation that numbed at least one part of her body. "He said he knew I'd be freaked out he was there, that's why he tried to let me handle things with Marty at first. I should be grateful he was there, I know. Because if he hadn't been…" Who was she kidding? She wouldn't need caffeine to stay awake. She'd be lucky if she slept all week.

"But it weirded you out that he was watching you," Kate filled in with a nod. "Me too. He seemed so nice. A little jumpy, but sweet. And sexy as all get out."

Hannah's eyebrows knit together. "You've met him?"

Kate nodded. "He must have heard me from upstairs when I came in. He came down to make sure someone hadn't broken in. I almost forgot. He brought down a bowl of fruit. He knew we never have any food in the house."

Hannah stared at the ceiling. The fruit was sweet. Her stomach lurched as she thought further. Was he listening to them right now?

"He is cute as can be. If his brother looks like him you should hook me up."

Hannah smiled at the idea, the first smile in hours. "The cop brother is married, but he has three more." Kate might actually be able to put Derek in his place.

Hannah threw her head back against the sofa cushions and squeezed her eyes tight. Her brain was a whir of activity, trying to make sense of Mason's behavior. And her own. She should be scared of him. He was skulking in dark parking lots, and this morning when he'd held the door closed she should have felt afraid. Instead all she could muster up for both incidents was minor annoyance.

Her mind knew what all the signs meant, but she just wasn't making the connection. Again. She had no common sense when it came to men.

When she felt Kate's fingers on her hand the lump in her throat grew. "I really like him. I know I'm being stupid, but I just can't help myself. Maybe the ladies at the coffee shop were right. Maybe he is stalking me."

"Honey, I think it's much more likely the cards came from Marty. You said you saw him again the same day you got the first card. Mason is a little overprotective; I'll give you that. But you don't throw the baby out with the bathwater."

As Kate squeezed her hand the tears broke free. Kate held her while she wept, releasing the terror she'd felt as Marty had approached. Her instincts had been wrong, again. She'd been so sure he wouldn't hurt her.

Hannah cried as long as she could, until Kate nudged her. "You've got twenty minutes to shower. I'll drive you in."

CHAPTER EIGHT

'DON'T ruin this for me," Kate pleaded, tossing a pair of jeans across the room. "Tomorrow I have to get up at the butt crack of dawn, take a puddle-jumper plane to the armpit of Oregon, and spend the entire week taking depositions about mold, eating really bad takeout. Put on the damned jeans. Where are your push-up bras?"

"I am not putting on sexy lingerie!" Hannah yelled, unzipping her dress and dropping it to the floor.

"And what do you call that?" Kate shot back, pointing at the stockings and garters.

"You know I can't stand pantyhose. This is practicality."

"I dare you to leave it on," Kate said as she slingshot a peach push-up bra at her friend. "Think of how powerful you'll feel."

Hannah looked down at her body and wondered where the power was supposed to come from. She hadn't seen Mason in two days and her body was throbbing for him. She unsnapped her comfortable mesh bra, replaced it with the push-up and surveyed the difference. Maybe with the right shoes…

"These are fantastic!" Kate squealed, pulling the come-get-me boots from the closet. "I must borrow them."

"Go ahead." Hannah slid jeans over her stockings.

Standing, she tucked her garter belt down beneath the waist-band and reached for the cream-colored sweater Kate tossed her way when she left the room. *So that's why she insisted on the push-up.* Hannah tugged the low-cut scoop neck back up her shoulders.

She was so tired. She'd worked open to close the last two days to keep from thinking about the incident, dodging questions from coworkers and mentally preparing for her seven a.m. breakfast tomorrow with the district and regional managers to discuss store safety.

And there were the messages from Marty's wife's divorce attorney threatening a subpoena. Thank goodness Kate was a lawyer. Kate promised to make it go away, and Hannah had to believe her.

She hadn't actually agreed to meet Mason and Derek for drinks tonight. Kate had stated it was happening, and Hannah had been too exhausted to argue. No matter how stupid it was, she wanted to see Mason. She hadn't returned a single one of his calls, but she wanted to be near him for a little while. Maybe this time his explanation would make sense.

"Is this first-date perfect or what?" Kate posed in her black cargo miniskirt and tiny black cardigan unbuttoned at the bottom, showcasing her flat belly to perfection.

"He isn't going to know what hit him." Hannah smiled, absorbing Kate's glee. Was it just a week ago she'd felt the same way? "Mason did warn you Derek talks a lot, right?"

"He showed me a picture when I went upstairs to make the arrangements."

As if that answered the question. She obviously needed more information. Kate could be brutal if unprepared.

"He's a psychology professor, so he thinks he knows what you're thinking."

"Hannah, I appreciate the heads up, but he's the first guy

with an advanced degree I've had a date with in two years. Men tend to get intimidated by my career. Just let me have this, okay?" Kate ticked Derek's attributes off on her fingers. "Cute guy, good family, he actually has a job and a brain."

"Fine." Hannah held up her hands and smiled. "Two hours and I have to be in bed."

"However you two decide to end your night is your business," Kate said, with a sassy smile.

"I'm not having sex with him." And she meant it. They needed to slow things way down.

"So says you," Kate said, bustling to the closet. "What shoes are you wearing?"

Kate was a complete idiot if she thought this was a good idea. Hannah hadn't been in the room with Mason two minutes and already she was thinking about sex. She'd almost dragged him back to her bedroom the moment he'd walked through the door.

But sex was not the problem with her and Mason. The issue was how fast things were moving, and sleeping with him again and again would only race them farther down a road she wasn't sure she wanted to travel with this man.

A man, she reminded herself, who thought it was okay to watch her in dark parking lots and check her apartment whenever he heard her roommate moving around.

Kate didn't think it was all that bad. But in light of the recent glaring example of her inability to judge character, Hannah appreciated Kate was getting to know him. Troy had distrusted him on sight. If Kate did the same thing Hannah would somehow find the strength to move past Mason McNally.

Kate seemed content to focus on the other McNally brother, pretending to find his jokes hilarious and his ideas insightful. So interesting, in fact, she hadn't even tasted her chocolate martini.

Hannah sipped her chardonnay and pretended to listen to Derek's latest adultery theory until she heard her name.

"It was Hannah's idea actually. Focusing on the type of women philandering men are attracted to has proved quite a puzzle." Derek shoved his glasses further up his nose.

"How was that Hannah's idea?" Mason asked as he removed all the condensation from the outside of his glass of beer.

"She wanted to know why married men are always attracted to her," Kate filled in.

Mason smirked and took a swig from his glass. "You didn't just tell her?"

Derek shrugged. "I can't be sure of anything."

"It's because you're hot," Mason said matter-of-factly.

Hannah bristled at the thought. Was that the only reason he bothered with her?

"That may be part of it." Derek nodded. "But I haven't found a pattern. The women are older, younger, college graduates, high-school dropouts, prettier, plainer. I haven't found the answer yet."

"And you won't if you keep looking at it like that." Kate finally attacked her martini.

"Like what?" Derek twisted in the booth to face her.

"Like it's a quantitative issue. Men don't cheat because the woman is thinner or younger or prettier. They cheat because of the way she makes them feel." Kate set her glass down emphatically on the table.

Derek's eyes bugged out of his head as Kate turned to him and continued her tirade. "How she appears to the rest of the world doesn't matter. As long as she makes him feel alive, makes him feel the things he can't or won't at home. He'll tell himself it's just about the sex, use the old 'a man has certain needs' line so often he begins to believe it. But it's rarely about sex at all. Men gravitate to Hannah because she's sexy and smart and driven, but they want to be with her because of what it means to have someone like her want them."

"That's what I said." Mason drained his beer, absently looking around the empty bar.

Hannah heard more than what he said. She had known Kate would put Derek in his place. Derek looked as if he was salivating. His research was obviously taking a whole new direction.

With Kate and Derek occupied in their mental battle Hannah excused herself and slid out of the booth, making a beeline for the ladies' room.

Once inside she checked the watch face embedded in the bangle at her wrist. She had promised Kate two hours, but surely she could back out a little early. The wine made her tired, and she had a big day tomorrow. She knew Mason wanted to talk, but if they did her mind would start spinning and she'd never get any sleep.

And she wanted to be sure she left Mason here at the bar. If he made it through the front door of her apartment Hannah knew she'd react exactly as he wanted her to. And sex was not the answer to anything. Time to make the short walk home, and be asleep within thirty minutes. Sounded like heaven.

Opening the door to make her excuses, Hannah ran smack into the broad chest she knew so well.

"Mason, what are you doing?"

"Waiting for you so I could apologize," he said quickly. "There are a million reasons a guy would come on to you, not just because you're smoking hot. I didn't mean to make you feel like an object."

"Should I thank Kate for that speech or did you do that already?" Hannah stared up at his intense expression, and tried to find her fear. The man was looming over her in a dark alcove at the back of a bar. He'd followed her back there, waited for her. Intuition should tell her to be afraid. Her instincts must be nonexistent, because she only felt an urge to wrap her arms around him and not let go.

It had been that way since the first time she'd seen him. No matter the situation, she couldn't be rational about him. Not when she'd thought he was married, not when he spied on her in parking lots, not when he loomed in dark hallways.

He huffed out a quick breath. "You have to give me a chance to explain."

Hannah stood her ground, crossing her arms across her chest. "Mason, I'm exhausted. I just want to go home and get some sleep. Alone."

"I haven't been able to sleep either. Every time I close my eyes I see the bottle shattering and I'm all the way across the parking lot." He ran his fingers through his hair. "I just need you to listen, okay? You're killing me here. You won't return my calls and it's obvious you're only here tonight because Kate made you come."

Hannah shrugged. "This is how it is with me during the holiday season." It was the truth. She had no time to spare this time of the year. That was why she never tried to date.

Mason peered down at her. "After what happened you could manage a phone call."

"I haven't figured out what I want to say to you." And she didn't want to answer the questions she was sure he had about Marty.

"I don't want you to say anything, just give me a chance to explain." He rubbed his hands across his face.

"I've been here all night."

"We've been at a table with them." Mason motioned to the booth Kate and Derek were in. *Were they kissing?*

"Mason, look!" Hannah leaned forward, absently touching his arm as she watched her friend canoodling in the booth.

Her heart melted. It had been so long since she'd seen Kate actually relax around a man. "She must actually like him. I thought she was doing this just to get us together."

"Me too. Let's give them some privacy." Mason pulled Hannah into an empty booth in the back. As she sat down he slid in next to her, trapping her against the wall. It was only now, forced to look at him, she noticed how hollow his eyes looked, almost haunted.

As he leaned in close his words washed over her like a waterfall. "I'm sorry. I wish I'd told you I was there instead of hiding in the parking lot. If I had, none of it would've happened. If I had just pulled up, you'd have been angry, but you'd have come with me, and he never could have gotten near you. Instead I waited and watched because I thought you'd be upset." His fingers pulled his hair forward. "I'm so sorry. It could have gone really, really wrong."

No kidding. Hannah straightened her posture. "Why were you there?"

"I had a bad feeling about those cards. I just wanted to make sure you got on the train. When I saw some guy talking to you I knew it was wrong, but I was thinking about pissing you off, not keeping you safe. Which was stupid."

Hannah laid her hand on his leg. "You did keep me safe. I shouldn't have stopped to talk to him."

Mason shook his head. "You couldn't have known, Hannah. Ryan said the guy didn't have any priors."

"Ryan, right. Your brother the cop, who has probably told your entire family I had an affair with a married man." Hannah's stomach lurched as she propped her elbows on the table and buried her face in her hands.

"He can't tell anyone, and he wouldn't either. You didn't know he was married. No one can hold that against you."

"He'll tell, and they will," Hannah said without looking up.

"Mason, I have to get past this stuff with Marty. I hate myself for it. I was so naive, so trusting." She took a deep breath, tilted her head to look at him, and dove in. "And I'm watching it happen again with you and it scares me. There are all these signs things are wrong with us. I ignored all the signs then, and I'm doing it again. I don't know if things can work out with us now."

Mason's eyes blazed like the center of a flame. "You cannot give him power over us."

"I know, I know. This is just all too much for me." Hannah's hands flailed about as she tried to make the chaos make sense. "Work is crazy, I have a meeting in the morning to discuss what happened that has me all worked up, and everything about us is just insane. My sister is freaking out, and she called my parents and now they all think I'm in way over my head with you. Which I can't really argue with. Ugh." She rested her head against the cold Formica of the table. "I didn't want to do this. I'll never get any sleep now."

"I didn't want to upset you," Mason said, gathering her up like a rag doll and pulling her into his arms. "I just wanted you to hear me." His fingers in her hair pulled the tension from her body. Maybe everything would work out.

"Let me take you home," Mason whispered in her ear.

The words cut through her like ice. She stiffened and pulled away. Of course, that was all he was after. That was all men ever wanted from her.

"I'm not having sex with you."

"How much did you drink?" Mason asked as they entered the apartment behind the women. Derek was definitely under the influence. The way he leered at Kate made Mason wonder if he needed to turn the hose on Derek before he molested Hannah's roommate.

"He's fine." Kate took Derek's hand, pulling him with her onto the couch.

Derek shot him a look he hadn't seen since high school. Derek had better know what he was doing because if he messed things up with Hannah—well, he was doing a good enough job of that on his own.

Mason looked around the room, but Hannah was gone. He stalked back to her bedroom, and, finding the door open slightly, he crept in, quietly closing it. "They sure hit it off," he said before turning around.

Hannah gasped, clutching the sweater she'd been wearing against her body. He should have worn nicer pants. Something pleated with a whole lot more breathing room. The seam in his crotch was cutting into him right now.

Defiantly she threw the garment to the floor, stamping her bare foot against the rug. "What are you doing in here?"

Mason reminded himself to breathe as he leaned back against the door. This was what she wore beneath her clothes? He brought his hand to his stomach as he sucked in breath. Flesh-colored stockings and garters and panties and a push-up bra. It was like Christmas for the eyes. He didn't even want to blink.

His mouth went dry with wanting. There was only one thing to wet it properly. He stepped to her and she held up her hand.

"Mason, I said what are you doing in here?"

"They…uh…you know, out there…" Damn. There wasn't enough blood in his brain to form a coherent thought.

"Derek and Kate? Really?" Hannah shrugged and put her hands on her hips.

Not good. Shrugging made her breasts bob up and down, up and down. He had to get out of these pants before they killed him. He undid the button and took another step.

Hannah's hand came up again. "Whoa there, cowboy. I made myself clear. I'm not having sex with you tonight."

Begging was definitely an option at this point. She'd just stepped out of a lingerie catalog, for goodness' sake. "Why are you...?" His hands waved up and down in front of her body, making him all too aware he was not connecting with her smooth skin.

"This is underwear, Mason. I'm not trying to seduce you. It's what I had on under the dress I wore to work today and I didn't have time to change."

"You always look like that under your clothes." It was a resigned statement, not a question. Was his voice an octave higher than normal?

"I suppose so," she said with a shrug. *Not another shrug.* Mason flopped down on the bed and covered his eyes.

"You're going to have to give me a minute here." He tried to think of something else. Something boring like Derek lecturing, except Derek was making out with Kate in the living room. No good. He heard Hannah rustling through her closet. If she pulled out another number like the green one the other night he'd embarrass himself right there.

He pressed his hands against his eyes harder. "Hannah, please, just put on something that covers you up."

"I'm not taking requests."

Even breathing was making it worse. The entire room had that clean laundry smell of her. The fifty states, in alphabetical order. That should work. The throbbing was slowly turning into an ache. He heard the door open and shut and he took a deep breath.

He needed to make sure they were still on for Thursday and then he'd give her the space she asked for. Which shouldn't be too hard because he was working every day until then anyway.

"Either they left or moved to her bedroom," Hannah whispered, closing the door behind her. Her face was scrubbed clean and her hair was pulled back into a ponytail. Mason was eternally grateful for the red knit top and flannel pajama pants. Though the body beneath them was barely disguised.

"Thank you," he said without getting up from the bed. Let her tell him to go one more time.

"You can thank my mother. This was my birthday present last year." She sat next to him on the bed, pressing buttons to set her alarm clock. "It's the only thing I own you'd consider appropriate."

He sat up next to her and kicked his shoes off and across the room.

Hannah stood by the side of the bed. "I said you weren't staying."

Mason raised a finger. "No, you said we weren't having sex."

Hannah shook her head and moved the pillows off of the comforter.

Putting his hands on his knees, he looked up at her. "What are we doing on Thursday?"

Hannah pulled her ponytail tighter. "Oh, Mason, honestly, I was planning on spending the whole day in bed. This whole thing has really taken it out of me."

Oh, yes. "Fine by me. Yours or mine?"

"You're incorrigible." Her smile made her eyes sparkle in the dim light. "I have a list of errands I have to run, but if you want maybe we could do dinner or something."

Or something? "I'm glad you can squeeze me in."

Hannah shrugged, getting up and pulling the comforter back as far as she could with him still on the bed. "This is how my life is during holiday."

"I know. I'm not crazy about it, but it isn't forever." He

pulled his sweater over his head and stood up, shucking his jeans and socks, tossing them on top of his shoes by the door.

"Mason," Hannah warned as he climbed into bed.

"What? You said no sex. I can behave, can you?" He patted the bed next to him and laid his head against the pillow.

Her eyes narrowed as she looked down at him. "I have to get up early. I have a breakfast meeting at seven."

Mason turned his head and smiled. She'd have to tell him to leave. "I have to be in to work by seven. I'll drop you off."

Her mouth opened to say something, another protest maybe? But she bit it back and climbed into bed beside him. She rolled, facing the outside edge with her back to him. Wrapping his arm around her waist, he pulled her against him.

"Mason, I can feel you." She wiggled her backside against his waning erection.

"Do that again and you'll feel more of me. You should feel it anyway; it's your fault. How did you expect me to react to what you were wearing?"

She giggled and he snaked his hand upwards. "Mason, hands off," she warned. Or was that a tease? He could never tell. He lowered his hand, stretching his fingers out so they splayed across her stomach, feeling every breath.

As he nestled her head beneath his chin he realized he might actually be able to sleep for the first time since that night. With her in his arms, he knew she was safe.

"Mason," Hannah whispered in the dark. "Did you plan this?"

"No." He smiled into her hair. "If I'd thought of it, I wouldn't be wearing underwear."

CHAPTER NINE

THE sound of creaking metal startled Hannah awake. In the darkness she stiffened and froze, waiting for the next sound.

"It's just bedsprings," Mason said, his voice gravelly and rough. His hand rubbed against her bare stomach. Some time during the night his fingers had crept beneath her shirt and waistband. "Go back to sleep."

Hannah let out the breath she was holding and relaxed down into the mattress. The creak of bedsprings grew more rhythmic, more insistent. Between that and the adrenaline rush of being woken there was no way she could sleep now. She checked the clock. Two-twenty. Too early to get up.

"You slept through the first two rounds; you can do it again if you try," Mason whispered in the dark as he pulled her closer.

She liked the feel of him, the way their legs intertwined in the night. She squeezed her eyes shut tight, but her brain kicked on in full force. "I'll go out to the living room so you can get some sleep." She tried to get up but he pinned her legs beneath his and held her firm.

"You need to sleep, Hannah."

"I know, I just can't now." She tried to muster up some fear. The man was holding her down in a bed. She should be afraid. All she felt was the low-level hum of arousal she always enjoyed around Mason. The feeling that switched off her common sense.

"Why?" She heard the pillow rustle as he pushed up on it behind her.

He relaxed his grip as she rolled over and looked up at him. "I don't know. My brain kicks on and I can't stop it."

"What do you usually do?"

Her heart stuttered in her chest. She usually dug one of her erotic romances out of her nightstand and read until she fell asleep or needed her vibrator. But she wasn't about to let him know that.

"Really?" he asked, as if he had read her mind.

He couldn't possibly know. "I didn't say anything."

"Your eyes," he whispered, kissing her forehead. "You know, since I'm here, if there is anything you'd like me to help you out with…"

How could he always see what she was thinking in her eyes? She shook her head. "Mason, I told you we are not having sex."

"No, you said we weren't having sex last night. It's technically morning, so you can make love with me and not break your word."

She bit her lip and searched his eyes. How had he used her eyes to read her mind, yet she could barely see his in the darkness? "Is that why you stayed?"

"No, not really. I didn't want to be away from you." His fingers began a lazy dance up and down her arm. "I never want to be away from you. I know you're busy, but if I'm going to live on five days a month then I need you to return my calls and let me come down once in a while." She watched his shoulders fall as the words came out, almost as if he were releasing himself from something.

"I warned you holiday was a crazy time for me." She splayed her hands across his chest, the fine hair tickling her palms. "But I am sorry I was avoiding you."

His body seemed to lighten on her apology. "That's okay. I'm already looking forward to your week off in February. Let's book a trip so we have something to look forward to."

She didn't have the heart to tell him if she got the promotion, as she was hoping, she wouldn't get the week in February. There'd be no vacation time for at least six months. "I should use the week to visit my folks in Arizona."

His finger stalled on her elbow. "You don't want me to go with you." It wasn't even a question.

She felt his discomfort. It was almost as if his heart hiccupped. "It's not that." Her parents would never approve of her bringing a boyfriend into their home. Not unless there was a ring on her finger. And even then, they'd have to sleep in separate rooms. She ran her hands up to cup his face, now rough with stubble. "February is a long time from now. I know it feels like more, but we're really only a few days into this relationship. Let's not make any promises we can't keep, okay?"

"I'm not going anywhere."

"You say that now."

Mason grabbed her wrists, pulling her hands between them and wrapping them with his own. "I'm not going anywhere. Hannah, I—"

His words were cut short by Kate's screams. "The penguins, yes, yes, the penguins!"

Hannah rolled onto her back as she tried to stifle the laughter racking her body.

"The penguins?" Mason asked, sitting up. "What the hell is he doing to her?"

"He's your brother," Hannah choked. "Kate collects penguins." A tear dropped from her eye. "I have to stop or they'll hear me."

Mason pushed himself on top of her, his face inches from hers. "They're a little preoccupied."

"Really? And here I thought they were dusting her figurines." Hannah erupted in laughter again as Mason pressed down on the bed, bouncing her beneath him. "Quit!" she yelped, trying to swallow her giggles.

His grin told her he wasn't planning on stopping. She wrapped her arms around his neck, her legs around his, and pulled him down on top of her. "Making me laugh is not helping me get back to sleep."

"Right," he said without moving. "I know something that will help you." His warm kiss on her neck did nothing to calm her down. Just as always, every nerve in her body went on red alert. Instinctively her legs tightened around him, her hand raked through his hair.

Before she lost all control she said, "Mason, this is not the answer to anything."

"Maybe it's the answer to everything." His hot breath tickled her neck as he made his way to the curve of her shoulder, her collarbone.

Molding her hands to his face, she raised his head to look at her and shook her head. Mason bit his lip and nodded, rolling off of her and to the side.

Her stomach sank as she watched him close his eyes and breathe deep. How could she make him understand when she barely got it herself? He jumped as she rested her hand against his chest. She pulled back, but he grabbed her hand, holding it where his heart was thumping. She could barely find her voice. "Every time I'm with you I get in deeper. I just need us to be about more than sex."

"We are," he whispered, stroking the back of her hand.

Hannah rolled to her side, pulling his hand with her. He wrapped himself behind her, warming her with his presence.

"Did you always have trouble sleeping?" he asked, running his fingers across her scalp and down her hair.

"Yeah. I would wake up early to be with my dad before he left for work. I was always listening for him. I think that made me a light sleeper."

"Are you still close with him?"

Hannah wondered if they ever had been. "He doesn't think I have a real job."

Mason's chest vibrated against her back as he laughed. "What does that mean?"

"He thinks it's something I'm doing until I get married and have babies." She thought of his words when she'd told him she was not coming to Christmas in Arizona, again. "Hannah, you work in a mall. Don't take yourself so seriously." Pointing out her last two stores had been freestanding wouldn't matter.

"Why does he think that?"

Hannah shrugged. Because that was how he thought the world worked. Because it never crossed his mind anyone might want anything else. Hannah blew away the heaviness of her emotions. If she kept talking about this she'd need to have sex with Mason just to feel better about herself. Instead she focused on his fingers, pressing them away from his palm as she traced their length.

Mason kissed her hair. "My dad still wants me to give up firefighting and join the force. Parents have dreams for us that don't actually jive with who we are."

"What you do makes a difference in people's lives. Your parents have to be proud of that."

"Are you okay with it? My job, I mean."

She was more than okay with it. It was incredibly sexy,

the way his whole career focused on helping other people. "Why wouldn't I be?"

"Some women have a problem with it. The schedule is rough. Twenty-four on and forty-eight off can make for a complicated home life."

"I'm hardly in a position to call anyone else's schedule crazy."

Mason spoke slowly, as if deliberately choosing his words. "We are highly trained and always very careful, but it can be dangerous if something goes wrong."

A chill ran down her spine at the thought. He hugged her closer as if he felt it too. She didn't even want to think about anything happening to him. She folded his hand between her own and brought it to her lips. "You just keep coming home in one piece and I'll be fine."

Mason slowly opened one eye and assessed the strange light glowing from Hannah's alarm clock. Every minute the light seemed to be getting brighter and brighter. What the hell?

He pushed up on his elbow. The entire thing was glowing as if it might explode. He rubbed his eyes as the light brightened again. It was pitch-black outside, but Hannah's bedroom was fast approaching dawn.

"We still have five more minutes," Hannah mumbled, scooting back into him.

"What is that thing?" Mason whispered, lying back down but not taking his eyes off the glowing box.

"My alarm clock? It's supposed to help me wake up gradually and reset my circadian rhythm. Christmas from my dad. He does all his shopping from those catalogs in the backs of seats on airplanes." All those words without even opening her eyes. She must be one of those freakish morning people. Finally, he'd figured out what was wrong with her. He could live with it.

"It gets even brighter?"

"I'll turn it off if you promise not to let me fall back asleep."

"I'll get used to it, I guess." Never going to happen. He'd been waking up to flashing lights since he was seventeen.

Hannah's hand reached from beneath the comforter and slapped the box. It immediately powered down, darkening the room once more.

"Thank you," he whispered against her hair, wrapping himself around her.

"Mason," she teased, wiggling her bottom against his morning erection.

"Find something you like?" He pressed himself against her.

"You have a one-track mind." She tucked the covers under her chin.

That was definitely not the "no" he'd heard all night. "You inspire me."

"I need to inspire you to get a new line. You've used that one before."

She didn't stop him as his hand drifted across her hip, under the waistband of her flannel pajama bottoms. He didn't stop, sliding the material down over the curve of her hip. *Damn.* She wasn't wearing any panties. Had she just been teasing him last night?

"Mason, we need to get up in four minutes." Her words hung in the air, but she didn't resist as he pushed the pants down past her thighs. Shucking his own boxers, he wrapped himself around her again, pushing her pants off the rest of the way with his foot. Brushing the hair away from her ear, he kissed her neck, savoring the scent of her soap that even now lingered on her skin. Hannah moaned and arched her back, pressing against him mercilessly.

His hand traveled under her shirt, palming her breast and squeezing, kneading until her breath went shallow. Hannah lifted her leg over his and arched back further, offering herself to him. Mason bit back a groan and released her breast, reaching over the top of her to throw open the nightstand drawer.

He fumbled around, searching for the box of condoms, not caring to imagine what some of the other objects he found might be. "Finally," he groaned as he snatched a condom from the box, rolled back and sheathed himself.

Snuggling against her, he worked his hand back to her breasts, brushing across each nipple in turn. "Hannah?" he whispered as he pulled her hair away from her face and began to kiss his way down her neck to where her shirt met her shoulder.

"Shh. I'm having the most amazing dream." She arched her back and rubbed against him. He slid his hand south from her breasts, over her tummy and into her dampened curls. She was so wet, so ready. He parted her lips and his length slid against them, absorbing her heat.

"Have this dream often?" he asked.

"All the time." Her voice was raspy from her shallow breathing.

He hissed as he slid inside of her, slipping his fingers on either side of her clit.

She hummed and leaned forward slightly, pressing back against him. He pulled out almost all the way, and then slid in again. He watched the comforter move as her hands found her breasts. In his mind he saw her tweaking each nipple.

"Hurry, Mason, I can't last," she rasped. Good thing, because neither could he. He quickened his pace, stroking her clit with each thrust. Her hands appeared over the comforter as she grabbed her pillow and buried her face in it.

The strength of her spasms shocked him, sending him over the edge immediately, milking him of all he had. He gathered her body against his, waiting for his mind to return to this world, while he stayed buried deep in her.

"Hey, Mason," Derek whispered as he knocked on the door and opened it without waiting for an answer. They were fine, covered more now than when they'd slept, but Hannah stiffened anyway.

Derek's head peeked in the room. "Wake up. I need to borrow some clothes. Where are your keys?"

"In my jacket pocket. It's on the chair in the living room."

"Thanks." Mason could swear he heard whistling as Derek closed the door.

"That did not just happen," Hannah squeaked as she buried her face in her hands.

"What?" His heart skipped. She couldn't mean them.

"That was too close."

"He didn't suspect anything. Trust me, Derek would say something."

"But we're lying here, together." She squeezed him with her inner muscles to accentuate her point. His body surged at the contact.

"It looks just like it did when we were sleeping." His hand traced the length of her thigh, the curve of her hip, the dip of her waist, up until he found her breast again.

"But if he came in even a minute before—"

"We wouldn't have known he was there." Mason laughed against her neck.

"This isn't funny, Mason. We shouldn't have started anything without locking the door first."

"Who knew you'd change your mind?" Mason edged his legs between hers once more.

"I'm only human." Her fingers wrapped around his, encouraging him. "I can't resist you forever." She released her hand. "You probably get that a lot."

No way was she shutting back down on him now. He began to thrust into her slowly, but fully. "You mean bright white lights, not caring if you ever breathe again, wondering if your nerves will ever be the same?" Already she was trying to hurry him, trying to quicken his pace. "That's not me doing that."

Hannah nodded furiously, her bottom lip sucked all the way into her mouth. "No, it is you. It's not like this for me. It's usually like ripples." Her hand dug into his hip as she urged him on. "Please, faster."

He kept up his leisurely pace, as if he could do this all day. Luckily she couldn't see the set to his jaw, the way his eyes were shut tight. A peek at any part of her would catapult him right over the razor's edge he was balancing on. "What's it like with me, Hannah?"

Her hand slipped from his hip. He knew where it was going. He pried her fingers from her swollen slit and held them firm. "Please" she whimpered, trying to tug either of their hands back down.

"Answer me. What's it like with me?"

She leaned forward and arched against him, meeting his slow thrusts with her own strokes. "Tidal waves." The words came out in breathy pants. How could either of them be this close already?

It was all just part of the magic. "It's not me, Hannah." His hand was finding the button to send her flying. "It's us. Us together. It's better because it's us."

Her head tilted back, the expression on her face robbing him of control. With her lips parted and her eyes closed she looked euphoric, blissful. Her muscles clenched around him and he had no choice but to hang on, enjoying the ecstasy they created together. He wanted to cry out, scream her name to the heavens, but knew that would ruin it for her. Instead he hauled her back up against him, holding her close until their breathing returned to normal. Amazing how it remained in cadence even after their lovemaking was finished.

"This is why you can't sleep over," Hannah teased.

"This is a reason in favor of my sleeping over."

Her hair tickled his cheek as she shook her head. "With you here I don't want to get out of bed."

"Why is that such a problem?"

"I have a breakfast meeting with my district and regional managers, three ramp-up seminars at three different stores, and a training class full of high-school sophomores."

He wrapped his fingers around hers. "You win. I have a trip to a preschool scheduled."

She rolled to face him, which left him amazingly aware he wasn't inside of her any longer. "You go to preschools?"

"Sure. Raise the ladder, let them climb on the truck. Preschool is where I decided I was going to be a firefighter." Teasingly he narrowed his eyes at her. "I'm not trading. I'll take toddlers over teenagers any day."

"What are you doing here?" Mason stopped so abruptly Hannah plowed right into the back of him. He didn't move. Peeking around him she saw Derek sitting on the couch with another man. A man who looked a lot like Mason, only bigger. This guy was a brick wall.

"Derek called me." Even his voice was big as it echoed in the small room.

Hannah tried to get a better look, but Mason had her fenced in the hallway. "Why?"

Derek reached for something on the table. "I found another card when I went to go upstairs."

Hannah closed her eyes at the words. *Another card.* Marty had been here, just steps away from where she slept.

Derek handed Mason a plastic bag. Inside was a card showing a picture of a naked, well-muscled male torso, a Santa hat leaving little to the imagination. "You can arrest him for this. Coming here violated the restraining order." Mason handed the bag back to Derek, but his feet stayed rooted.

"Probably not," the big man said. Hannah saw Mason's shoulders tense as he stepped toward the man.

"Then why are you here, Junior? If there's nothing you can do but make more sorry excuses." Even in her nervous state Hannah couldn't help but smile at someone calling this behemoth Junior.

"Watch your mouth, Francis. I told you why we couldn't hold him."

Derek stood between the men calmly, as if there was nothing frightening about standing between two towers of testosterone.

"Someone want to fill me in?" Hannah said, stepping into the room from the hallway.

The three men turned to face her as she crossed her hands across her chest. She wanted answers, and quickly because she had to get on with her day. Mason spoke first, but turned his words on the big man. "This is my older brother, Mike. He's a captain at the precinct that released that bastard as soon as he was sober. Some bullshit about no priors and a shortage of beds."

Hannah hadn't wanted to know what happened to Marty. She also hadn't wanted to make this kind of a first impression on so many members of Mason's family.

Mike shook his head. "The cards aren't him, Mason."

Mason spun on his heel and pushed Derek aside. Derek merely rolled his eyes and stepped between them again. "Why? Because he said so?"

"No, because I've been tracking his credit cards and cell phone. He's in Maryland trying to patch things up with his wife."

Hannah just wanted to get to work. Get to someplace where she was in control of what was going on around her. And even if today started with a meeting with both the district and regional managers about the very incident she was trying to avoid thinking about, she could take it. So long as her head wasn't being filled with more speculation about the damned cards.

Mason, Derek and Mike were huddled around the coffee table exchanging theories. Mason still suspected Marty, but kept mentioning Troy—her brother-in-law!—and Jeremy Tolliver. Hannah didn't mention that she'd be spending the next three days with Jeremy. Mason might come unhinged.

Derek was concerned the cards might be meant for Kate. She thought a neighbor was probably responsible. A neighbor annoyed by midnight screaming about penguins, no doubt. Hannah smiled and decided that was the option she was sticking with. It was six in the morning—much too early for conspiracy theories.

"Dad thinks it's probably a woman," Mike asserted. Hannah turned, her tea sloshing onto the floor, narrowly avoiding the front of her suit.

"You said he wouldn't tell," she hissed at Mason. His whole damned family knew about the biggest mistake of her life. Yeah, they were going to just love her.

"What?" Mason looked at her, puzzled. "You mean Ryan? He didn't; I did."

Hannah felt the color rising from her neck to her hairline as she slammed the mug against the counter. "You what?"

"Come on, honey, let's go grab some bagels at the coffee

shop." Kate grabbed her arm and jerked her to the door. She was still fuming as the door closed behind her and she found her coat thrust into her hands.

"What did you do that for?"

"You were about to lay into him, that's what for." Kate stepped quickly across the landing and down the stairs. Hannah had to hurry to keep pace with her as they hit the street. "When you're scared, you get mean," Kate said as the cold morning air hit their faces.

Hannah thought about arguing, but didn't bother. She stuffed her hands deeper in her pockets and trudged beside her friend for the block until they reached the coffee shop. While the clerk bagged the bagels for Kate, Hannah tried to ignore the smell. She walked to the window, running her fingers across the velvet of the chair she had sat in the last time she was here. She smiled, remembering the way Mason's kiss had made her toes tingle.

"I have to know," a voice said from behind her. "Is he stalking you or not?" Hannah turned, recognizing the brunette from the writing club she'd been eavesdropping on that morning.

Hannah smiled at the ridiculous situation. "Are you writing the romance or the suspense?" If the woman was going to be nosy, then she could be too.

"Romance. At least it's supposed to be, but I'm stuck."

Kate walked behind the woman, arching her eyebrow at the conversation.

"Then even if I say he's not, it probably won't help you."

The woman shook her head and grinned. "I'm glad, though. You two look great together."

Hannah smiled, leaving with Kate and the bagels.

"What was that about?"

"Nothing," Hannah said with a wave of her hand, digging into the bag for a bagel. Still warm.

"Take my car while I'm gone. It's safer than the train."

Hannah had statistics to prove the train was actually safer, but they didn't factor in greeting-card droppers. In any case, if she had a car she wouldn't have to ride with Jeremy between stores.

"Thanks." She meant the save from snapping at Mason, the bagel, the car, everything.

"Don't thank me. This way I can make Derek drive me to the airport."

Hannah grinned, realizing she'd forever link Derek to screaming penguins. "Are you coming home this weekend?"

As she punched the code and swung open the door to the building Hannah noticed Kate's expression change. "I already booked my ticket to Vegas. Remember, I was going to try and have some fun."

"Don't come back on my account," Hannah said, ascending the stairs.

"I wouldn't, honey. You can take care of yourself."

"Oh, I see how it is." Reaching their door, Hannah turned back to face her friend. "You want more of whatever Derek was doing with those penguins last night."

CHAPTER TEN

HANNAH pretended the day was normal, smiling as she took her seat at the restaurant table opposite the two people controlling the rest of her career. Put aside the morning spent pondering stalker theories with Mason and his brothers. There was no room for that here, now.

Dean Curtis checked his watch as she sat down. She still had three minutes until she was technically late, but on time was out of character for Hannah. But then, so was dealing with police captains in her home before breakfast.

As he was District Manager, meetings with Dean were nothing out of the ordinary. Meetings with Regional Manager Judy Miller were rarer. The woman oversaw five districts in four states. Judy's warm smile put Hannah at ease, helping her to school her features into the confident mask she wore so well. Hannah had liked Judy from the day they'd met at a career fair in college. Judy had recruited Hannah to Mendelssohn's and followed her career every step of the way.

"Are you ready for today?" Dean asked, sipping the coffee already on the table.

"Absolutely." Hannah nodded. "I've had the presentation organized for weeks."

"You always get so excited for holiday. I'm sure you'll spread your enthusiasm around, just as always." The older woman smiled.

A waitress appeared, taking their orders and removing the coffee from Hannah's place. Hannah's cell phone rang to life, rattling her nerves. She wondered about answering it, but saw it was the store and decided to chance their disapproval.

"Hannah Daniels."

"When are you coming in?" Gary's voice sounded tinny and frantic across the line. Hannah knew she'd been placed at the store to compensate for Gary's weaknesses, but the man relied on her more and more every day. It must be nice to be able to delegate your entire job to someone else.

Hannah chose her words carefully, aware of who was listening in as she replied. She knew Gary was already on thin ice. She wanted credit for all she was doing, but she didn't want to sink another man's career either. She hoped it sounded that way.

Without asking about the phone call, Judy turned to Dean. "Call Gary. Drop in while Hannah is away so you can get a grip on how he's handling things without her."

Dean nodded, grabbed his phone and excused himself from the table. Hannah hoped some day she'd be able to speak with such authority and command so much respect.

"Your boyfriend was late picking you up?" Hannah jumped in her skin at Judy's words. *Let's just cut to the chase.* She didn't have to ask what the other woman was referring to.

"I wasn't sure he was coming."

Judy nodded. "You knew the man?"

"Yes. We dated a year and a half ago."

"The police are taking care of it?"

Hannah couldn't help the corners of her mouth turning up

as she thought about the level of police involvement. "Of course. They aren't holding him, but he's out of state right now."

"Can he do that? Go out of state while charges are pending?"

Hannah hadn't even thought to ask Mike that. "I'm really more interested in putting it all behind me."

"Good. Don't discuss it at work again. Just say it's been taken care of. I got the memo on your conference call over the weekend. Good call, making sure building security is available for walk-outs at closing. Like you said, we're paying for it with our rent."

"Thank you." Hannah drank in the compliment from her mentor like fine wine.

"You don't have to answer this, but is it serious, with your boyfriend?"

Hannah nodded. It had felt damned serious this morning.

"How is he handling the holiday schedule?"

"Well, actually, he's a firefighter, so he understands wacky schedules."

"That does help. My husband was in his residency while I was an assistant. Have you warned him what will happen when you get your own store?"

"It gets worse?" Hannah said with a laugh.

"More responsibility. But you have more control over the schedule. It's actually a good time to have small children. You'll manage it, just as I did."

Her stomach flipped. "If I get my own store."

Judy grinned from ear to ear. "Galleria in mid-February. Jim's accepting the district manager position in Northern California. I want you to take all your vacation time first. That will pull you out of Westside early January."

"Are you offering me the promotion?" Hannah's heartbeat thrummed in her ears.

GET FREE BOOKS and a FREE MYSTERY GIFT WHEN YOU PLAY THE...

Just scratch off the silver box with a coin. Then check below to see the gifts you get!

SLOT MACHINE GAME!

YES! I have scratched off the silver box. Please send me the four FREE books and mystery gift for which I qualify. I understand I am under no obligation to purchase any books, as explained on the back of this card. I am over 18 years of age.

P6EI

Mrs/Miss/Ms/Mr	Initials	
		BLOCK CAPITALS PLEASE

Surname _____

Address _____

_____

Postcode _____

7	7	7	Worth FOUR FREE BOOKS plus a BONUS Mystery Gift!
🍒	🍒	🍒	Worth FOUR FREE BOOKS!
♣	♣	♣	Worth ONE FREE BOOK!
🔔	🔔	🍒	TRY AGAIN!

Visit us online at www.millsandboon.co.uk

The Reader Service™ — Here's how it works:

Accepting the free books places you under no obligation to buy anything. You may keep the books and gift and return the despatch note marked 'cancel'. If we do not hear from you, about a month later we'll send you 6 brand new books and invoice you just £2.80* each. That's the complete price - there is no extra charge for postage and packing. You may c̲ at any time, otherwise every month we'll send you 6 more books, which you may either purchase or return to us - the choice is yours.

*Terms and prices subject to change without notice.

"Absolutely. You've earned it, Hannah. Dean will tell Gary today, and the paperwork is being processed. I assumed you'd be accepting."

Hannah barely resisted the urge to leap across the table and hug the woman. *She'd done it.* Her own store.

The second the meeting was over she dialed her cell phone at a frantic pace. This news was just too good to sit on.

But nobody she told shared her enthusiasm.

Even Molly had to feign happiness. She said all the right things. But she also asked Hannah way too many questions about the future.

Hannah's answers surprised herself. Judy had it all: the husband, children and a successful career. She could too, if she prioritized and worked hard. With her thirtieth birthday approaching, her biological clock had started ticking like a time bomb. And Mason had her dreaming about baby boys with deep blue eyes. Hannah shook her head at the notion. She was getting way ahead of herself.

Kate would be happy for her, if she ever checked her voice mail. Maybe Mason too. Hannah busied herself with work, pretending it didn't matter.

She finished the last of her mural on the dry-erase board and looked about the room. She was all set for the seminar with twenty minutes to spare. And still no Jeremy. That might have vexed her two days ago, but, now that she had the promotion, sharing credit with him didn't bother her.

Hannah jumped as her phone chirped to life. She leapt across the room and dug it out of her bag. Checking the caller ID, she felt warmed from the inside out. *Mason.*

"Miss me already?"

She bit her cheek, wondering if she should chance his reaction. "I just worried you might have been late to work, with all the commotion this morning."

"I'm more worried about being away from you until Wednesday night. What time will you be home?"

Hannah's spirit lightened. "Early, like dinnertime. My store manager is taking over the training classes."

"He's taking your teenagers? Lucky you."

"Very." Dean was using the training to help Gary with his teaching skills. Hannah swallowed hard. To heck with it, she wanted to know how he'd react. "I have something to celebrate."

"Me too."

"Should we wait and share, or can I tell you mine now?"

"We should wait. Anticipation makes everything better."

"Are you sure you can't come with me this weekend?" Kate whined, her pen clicking in the background.

Hannah kicked off her shoes and shrugged off her blazer. She was so glad to be home. "I'm sure. Calling in sick to work isn't my style. It causes more problems than it solves. You'll have a great time anyway."

"I'd better. This week has been just awful. I deserve a good time."

"Ask Derek to go with you." Hannah smiled at the sound of her best friend's voice and curled up on the couch.

"Honey, I don't trust myself in Vegas with that man."

Hannah tried not to laugh. "What does that mean?"

"It means I should have tried this whole younger man thing years ago."

"He's younger than you? But he's older than Mason."

"Only by thirteen months. Twins the hard way, he calls it. Anyway, he's six months younger than me." Kate let out a low whistle. "It's really working for us."

"It was certainly working for you on Sunday night."

"You don't know the half of it." Kate giggled. Kate never giggled.

"Are you giggling?"

"I can't explain what that man does to me. He makes me feel powerful and yet feminine at the same time. It's as if I'm constantly excited to be alive."

"Wasn't that the point you were trying to make to him? That affairs are not about sex, but about the way the other person makes you feel."

"I thought so. And I still think I'm right, but he has me thinking about all sorts of other things."

That was what Hannah worried about. "Some of his theories getting to you?"

"He's actually very insightful, Hannah. His family inspired a lot of his research. All through grad school he was working on sibling theories. Even though he's the second oldest, Derek has always felt like the middle child because he and Mason were so close in age, and Ryan didn't come until five years later."

Hannah leaned back on the couch and sighed. She didn't want to hear Derek's psychobabble second hand. Or find out Mason's family history from someone else.

Hannah's face scrunched up as she recognized why. She was jealous, plain and simple. Kate and Derek didn't have family throwing up roadblocks or a psycho stalker ex-boyfriend to get in the way of getting to know each other.

"Can you believe that? Three days that turned into almost forty years. It explains a lot about them, don't you think?"

Why hadn't she been listening? "How so?" was all she could think to say.

"How they can just trust their instincts. I still think it's kind of like hitting the lottery and spending your winnings on more tickets, but it's romantic as all get out. I mean, knowing from that first few moments together this is the person you were meant to be with. It's wild."

What exactly was Kate rambling about now? "They call that lust."

"That's what I told him. Derek thinks amazing sex is the most effective way to jump-start a relationship."

And she bought that line? "He would."

"Believe me, it was my pleasure. I don't know what has come over me. The man has me going from being a relationship skeptic to an advocate for love at first sight."

Hannah's breath caught in her throat. "Do you really think you're in love with him?" Her heartbeat echoed in her ear against the silence of the telephone receiver.

"Honey, I don't know," Kate said slowly. "I don't know what this feeling is, but I don't want it to stop."

But it would, and Kate needed to be prepared. "What if it's just a sexual spark? A feral heat that will burn out as quickly as it was ignited. Or an obsessive fascination. Or maybe a hero complex he has about wanting to save you from the cards. He said they could be targeting you."

Kate's laughter rang across the phone lines. "Who are you trying to convince here, honey? Me or you?"

"I thought I heard you down here." Mason brushed past Hannah, and into her apartment.

Awareness spiked. He'd been listening for her. "Just how much can you hear from up there?"

"Not much, really." His eyes scanned the room. "I heard the door more than anything else."

She'd been talking on the phone with Kate for at least a half hour since she'd opened the door. Talking to Kate and realizing how little she knew about Mason. Maybe if they just stayed out of bed, she might not feel at such a loss. "Something I can help you find?"

Mason turned, his eyes rolling over her so slowly her stomach clenched, then released into a pool of heat. She was still wearing her skirt and camisole from work today. Not exactly designed to thrill. But she saw from the way his eyes darkened it worked for him on some level.

He crossed the room until he was standing toe to toe with her. "Hmm, let me see," he said, examining the top of her head.

"What are you doing?"

His fingers undid the clip holding her hair in place, letting it cascade down her back. Her eyes closed as he raked the strands with his fingers.

His hands formed around her face, tilting her mouth up to receive his. Her lips instantly parted. She took in the scent of him, the smell of the soap from his shower. The shower where they—

Mason pulled away, but held her face. Hannah's eyes fluttered open, her conscience mocking her attempt to stay out of Mason's bed.

"There's my girl." Mason's thumbs brushed against her cheeks.

"This is your way of saying you like my hair better down?"

"Up, down, it doesn't matter, as long as you look at me like this." He leaned in for a kiss so quick Hannah felt bereft when he stepped away.

Which was good, exactly what she needed. Why did it make her want to tackle him to the ground?

"Do you want to go first?"

"Hmm?" She licked her lips. She could knock him right into the upholstered chair and—

"You said you had something to celebrate too."

"Oh, that." Her family had stamped out Hannah's excitement. Her mother had come right out and told her she worked too much to make a good wife for any man. Actually said the words, "A man wants a woman to be home when he is, Hannah."

Her father hadn't been much better. "As long as it keeps you busy." She wanted to hold onto what little joy she had left from the promotion. If Mason acted the way her parents had even that would be lost.

"What's your news?"

Mason sat in the upholstered chair, making Hannah suck the inside of her cheek. "I get to sit for the fire inspector's exam. It's a tiny bit more money, moderately better hours, and a whole lot less dangerous."

His toothy grin was sexy as hell, but Hannah tried to focus. "I thought you liked your job."

"I do, I really do. And a position probably won't come open for a while. But I've always wanted to be an inspector; it's just not the job you start out with." His face was so animated as he spoke Hannah knew he was telling the truth. "There is a lot to learn that can only be done hands-on. That's one of the reasons why I do so many volunteer hours at rural departments. The more you've seen, the more you know. And I like the puzzle-solving aspect. Plus you can't be a firefighter forever. It's a physically demanding job."

Hannah rolled her eyes. "You're in great shape."

"Really? You think so?" He waggled his eyebrows at her. "Then why are you standing all the way over there?"

Hannah stepped carefully across the rug, not wanting to snag her stockings. Standing next to his chair, she wondered if she wanted to chance telling him at all. Maybe celebrating his news was enough for one night.

"You're not happy about it?" The back of his hand skimmed

her skirt. "My mother was through the roof at the thought I wouldn't be running into burning buildings instead of out."

Hannah smiled, realizing he actually cared what she thought. "I meant what I said. I'm fine with that aspect of your job. I want you to do what makes you happy."

"Good answer," he said, dragging her down to his lap. He nuzzled her ear, causing her to curl into him. "What's your news?" His hot breath tickled all the way down her spine.

She turned and kissed him. Running her hands down his chest, she whispered, "Let's just celebrate your news." Her hands lifted the material of his sweater up over his abs. She pressed her hands flat against his skin and ran her palms all the way up to his shoulders.

Sucking in a breath, he covered her hands with his own. "What happened?"

When he reacted the way the others did she wouldn't want to be with him. And though she'd thought that was what she wanted only five minutes ago, that was not what she wanted now. She wanted *him*. Now. She leaned closer, capturing his lips with hers. The fever in her kiss heated the room. She reached around and unzipped her skirt.

Mason pulled her face away from his. "Tell me what happened. You were so excited."

She still was excited, but she didn't want to risk his reaction. Not when she still felt so fragile about her parents' response. She tried to kiss him again, but his hands held her still.

"You won't tell me?" The hurt in his eyes cut straight to her soul. She didn't want to save herself pain if it meant causing him any.

She rolled her head back on her shoulders, releasing herself from his grasp. She straightened her posture and looked him straight in the eye. "I got promoted to Store Manager."

"No way!" The twinkle in his eyes matched his grin. "You said you wouldn't know until after the holiday season. Wow! Congratulations!" He pulled her close, looking genuinely happy.

"Where?" He released her.

"The Galleria."

His eyes widened. "As in four blocks from here?"

She nodded. She'd never seen so many of his teeth.

"That's fantastic! Think of all the commute time you'll save. It might wash out some of the extra hours you'll have to put in."

"You're okay with that?" How was someone who'd only known her a few weeks more supportive than the family who'd known her forever? And why did it feel as if she'd known Mason longer than any of them?

His eyes rolled. "Hannah, I'd be a hypocrite to complain about your schedule. Besides, with your own store you'll have more control so things will run smoother."

Was that confidence in her abilities she heard? She let out a breath she'd been holding for two days. "I haven't told you the best part. I get to take my vacation time before I start. I'll probably get three weeks in January."

"Three weeks? New Zealand."

Hannah shook her head. "Excuse me?"

"Let's go to New Zealand, or Australia. Scuba dive the Great Barrier Reef."

"I can't scuba dive, Mason. I can barely swim."

"Snorkel, then. You can snorkel. It's just like floating in an aquarium." He squeezed her tighter. "You'll love it."

"Floating in an aquarium." And the appeal of that? "I'll think about it."

"It will be great. I have some magazines upstairs. I'll go get them." He shifted to get up, but stopped when Hannah turned his cheek with her finger.

How she wanted this man. "Is that really what you want to do right now?"

Mason cleared his throat. "I guess not. I thought we were going to have dinner to celebrate."

"Mason. I've waited two days for someone to give me that reaction. Believe me, you want to be rewarded for it."

The perfect woman. No doubt about it. Smart, beautiful, good job, and wanted to reward him for nothing. Couldn't get much better.

Except he didn't want her to make love with him as a reward. He wanted to know who the jerks were who rained on her parade. "What reaction were you getting?"

"It doesn't matter." But it obviously mattered to her, so it mattered to him.

"Yes, it does."

"My family doesn't see it as the opportunity I—we do."

Mason winced. How could anyone not appreciate her? "This goes back to them not taking your career seriously."

Hannah nodded. "I was worried you might react the same way."

Mason shook his head and gathered her close. "Honey, I want you to be happy like you were that morning on the phone, and just now. I'm in support of whatever it takes to get you to that place."

Hannah's eyes narrowed. "Even if it means I have less time for you."

"You'll make time for me." He'd make sure of it.

Like summertime in the beginning of winter, her kiss was warm and inviting. Warm and sweet and tender, but with an undertow that pulled a man straight to the dark side. He could kiss her all day, if he could control himself.

Which he never seemed to be able to do around her.

Hannah walked into a room and he was looking for escape routes, dark corners, and easily removable pieces of clothing. Like the textured black skirt she'd already unzipped. His hand slipped across the slippery fabric of her top and slid down the opening of her skirt. Her top went down as far as her skirt was open.

"Do you want me to take it off?" Hannah pulled away, her eyes dark and hazy.

He could only nod, hoping she meant more than just the skirt. As she rose from his lap he pulled his sweater over his head, then watched as she wiggled out of the skirt. Her top actually fell with a lacy hem at mid thigh. A slip.

The seam of his jeans dug into him as if it had been cinched. She stepped forward and pushed his legs together. Not the best idea, but he wasn't about to tell her to stop as she stepped her legs on the outside of his, moving up until their torsos were almost touching, spreading his legs in a temporary release.

She took his hands in hers, placing them on the outside of her thighs. She pulled them upwards, his palms rubbing the silk of her stockings until he found the edge, and her bare thigh. She was walking around in lingerie and thigh-highs. The perfect woman. He continued the journey until he found her panties. As he began to pull them down her hands stopped him.

"You don't have to," she whispered. She led his hand to her center urging him forward to find her meaning. Crotchless panties.

He groaned and looked into her eyes. They sparkled, daring him to continue. He held her gaze as he slipped first one finger inside of her, then two. She bit her lip as he curled them and pressed his thumb on her clit. When he tried to stroke her she stilled his hand and removed it. Without breaking the gaze he brought his fingers into his mouth and sucked, hard.

"You are some kind of tease."

"Who's teasing?"

Hannah shook her head. "That's not what I want right now." Her fingers found the button of his jeans and he lifted his hips to help with the straining zipper. He was grateful as she carefully removed him from his boxers before shoving them down with his jeans. He tried to kick them off, but remembered he still had his shoes on. Other realities flooded in, like the fact he didn't have a condom.

"Hannah, let's go to the bedroom."

She shook her head. "Why?"

"Because that's where the condoms are."

"I have on crotchless panties and you don't even bring a condom? There is a severe imbalance of power in our relationship."

"It will never happen again, I promise."

"It had better not. You stay here, I'll get one."

"Here? Why?"

"I have a thing about that chair," she tossed over her shoulder as she sashayed to her bedroom. The chair? Whatever she wanted. His shoes, socks, pants and underwear flew toward the door.

The click of heels on hardwood alerted him Hannah was on her way back. Except she hadn't been wearing any shoes before. He'd had to lift her face and bend down to kiss her earlier.

The shoes in question were sparkling ruby red with at least three inches of stiletto heel. And they did amazing things for her already shapely legs. As she neared he reached for the condom packet she held in her right hand, and then froze when he saw what was dangling from her left. She had to be joking.

"We don't need handcuffs, Hannah."

She swung the metal cuffs from her finger. "The power is not balanced in our relationship, Mason."

He gritted his teeth. He'd purposely taken the condom out of his wallet. He was always trying to jump her as it was. "I told you, it won't happen again."

She sat on his lap, rubbing her satin-clad hip against his hardness. "I promise, you will love it."

He grasped her wrist as she grabbed for his. "No, Hannah. We don't need props."

"Don't you trust me?" she pouted.

She couldn't possibly expect him to fall for that. "Of course I trust you, it's those things I don't trust. How many times have you heard about someone losing a key?"

Hannah held them up and pressed a button on the side, releasing the catch. "Relax, they were a prop from one of my sister's displays at her lingerie store. And your hands will just be behind the chair, not on anything."

"Is this for you or for me?"

Hannah shrugged. "Maybe it's for me. It's a fantasy I never dreamed I'd be brave enough to act out." She leaned closer, whispering in his ear. "I tell you what. You play with me now, and after dinner I'll do anything you want."

His pulse quickened. "Anything?"

"Within reason."

He shook his head. "Anything."

He watched her neck as she swallowed hard. "Fine. Anything."

CHAPTER ELEVEN

HAD she got to his apartment yet? Mason thought about checking at Hannah's place on the way upstairs, but decided against it. No point in letting her know just how long it had taken him if he didn't have to. Pushing the door open, he dropped the take-out bag on the counter, pulled out the tea lights, and kept going.

He needed one last look at the bedroom. Just to make sure he hadn't forgotten anything. And to scatter the tiny candles about the room. If he hadn't had to wait for the food he would have skipped this step entirely.

Hearing the knock at the door, he scooted out of the room, closing the door behind him. He hoped she'd try it, but it didn't matter if she backed out. As long as she stayed the night in his bed.

He pulled the two taper candles out of the bag and stuck them in the skinny shot glasses from the cupboard. He set them on the table and lit them as she knocked again.

He killed the lights and dashed for the door. Opening it, he raised an eyebrow at her coat.

"Did you take a walk while you were waiting for me to get back?"

"Something like that." She stepped past him into the room. "It smells like a Chinese restaurant in here."

"There's good reason for that." He kissed her cheek and scrambled to the kitchen, cursing himself for napping instead of eating lunch. He was starving. The sooner they ate, the sooner they could get on with the evening.

"What do you have planned for tonight?" Her hands dug into her coat pockets.

"First we eat." He pulled the take-out boxes from the bag without looking up. "I'm hungry and we'll need our energy for later." For *anything*.

His grin faded as he looked up, finding her gloriously naked in the middle of his living room, candlelight licking over her body. God, but she was impossibly beautiful. Her kind of beauty made his knees weak, his pulse race, and his mouth water. He loved the way she made him feel.

"Later," he growled, dropping the box of fried rice on the counter.

"No, you're right. First we eat."

"With you naked? I don't think so."

Her hand flat against his chest stopped him. For now.

"Yes, with me naked. And you fully clothed. I told you earlier. We need to reset the balance of power in this relationship."

His hands wrapped around her waist and pulled her flush against him. To hell with food. He'd just eat her. "You already did."

As he leaned in to kiss her she stalled his lips with her finger. "Are you sure you want this to be your *anything*? Because that's definitely a one-shot deal."

The gleam in his too-blue eyes made anticipation curl in her lower belly. He wanted her. So bad it radiated off of him. And she had an insatiable desire for this man that defied explanation. She removed her finger from his lips and parted her own, greedy for what he had in store for her.

"You're right; I don't want to waste it. Who knows when you'll offer me *anything* again?" He released her and stalked back to the kitchen. He had to know what he was doing to her.

She followed him, wishing she hadn't kicked off her sandals. Why hadn't she worn the stilettos from earlier, or better yet the come-get-me boots? Yes, he wouldn't have walked away from those.

He poured water into a teakettle and set it on the stove, piled the food onto plates and set them on the table. Hannah wondered if she'd actually be able to go through with her dare and eat naked. It sounded like a great dieting trick.

She'd intended to end her trepidation about agreeing to *anything* with her naked-beneath-her-coat stunt. She'd seriously underestimated his will-power. Time to turn up the heat.

She stepped into the kitchen and cocked her hip on the counter. "Where did you go?"

"Go? Oh, you mean for dinner." He didn't look at her, keeping his hands busy with opening and closing take-out boxes. "Jen Dynasty. It's only three blocks away and they have really good Kung Pao and I remembered you like spicy." His hands gripped the counter as she stepped closer.

"I like hot, but spicy is good too."

His knuckles went white, but still he didn't look at her. "There's a difference?"

She turned his face with a finger to look at her. "Hot is you and me. Spicy is you and me and a pair of handcuffs." His eyes threw sparks right through her as his breath came out in a rush that bordered on a growl.

His eyes closed as she traced his lips with her fingers. But still he made no move to touch her.

"You must really want *anything*."

Mason nodded. "I do. But if you touch me again I'm never going to make it."

She wanted him so bad she could taste it. And he'd just admitted he was hers if she tried anything. Curiosity stopped her from pouncing and taking him here in the kitchen. If he was willing to wait, *anything* must be pretty damned fantastic.

The teakettle whistled to life behind them and Mason jumped into motion. He pulled a teapot out of a cupboard and dropped some teabags in before filling it with water.

"You actually own a teapot?"

Mason nodded. "I got it a few weeks ago when I gave up coffee." She just made out the side of his grin as he placed everything on the table.

He couldn't have given up coffee just because she didn't like the vile brew. "Because of what happened at the coffee shop?"

"Yes, because of what happened at the coffee shop." He winked at her. *Winked?* He motioned for her to sit down, waiting until she did before he sat. God bless his mother.

Hannah was thankful he hadn't bothered with chopsticks as she surveyed the plate. Kung Pao chicken, orange beef, chow mein and white rice. All things she'd have been wearing if she'd even attempted it. Which served to remind her she wasn't wearing anything at all.

"Can I ask you about this *anything* you have planned?" Hannah lifted a forkful of rice to her mouth. Jasmine rice. Her favorite.

"It's more of a show than a tell." He was careful to keep his eyes on hers.

"Sounds interesting." She leaned back in the chair, changing his view. He slammed his eyes shut; she hid her smile when he opened them again. "I'm just wondering what to expect. You know, if I need to be prepared."

He shook his head. "It will never happen again. And for the record I didn't have a condom on purpose."

She cocked an eyebrow his way. "That's an interesting excuse."

"It was my lame attempt not to jump you the moment I saw you. Didn't work, so from now on I'll always be prepared."

"What a good boy scout. Trying to earn your safe-sex merit badge?"

"You go ahead and keep teasing me." His eyes twinkled before he dropped his head and concentrated on shoveling food into his mouth. Passion came out in everything he did. Work, food, sex. She slid her bare foot across the floor, finding his ankle and rubbing up the leg of his jeans. His fork froze in the air, but he didn't look up. "Hannah." His voice held a warning.

"Yes?" she asked sweetly, picking up the mug of tea he poured her. Jasmine tea. She sipped again. The same blend she drank at home.

"Are you about done?"

"Done with what?" She ran her toe higher. He caught her foot between his knees, making her gasp as he held it there.

"Done taunting me." His voice was low and gravelly. "Quit trying to back out."

"Mason, I'm naked in your kitchen. I hardly call that backing out."

"You're trying to run the show, but this is my turn. My fantasy. I played along and so should you."

"You enjoyed yourself."

"And so will you if you just relax." Mason rubbed his hands across his thighs, still holding her foot captive. "Hannah, those handcuffs were a one-time deal. Well, maybe not one time, but at least until you make District Manager."

When she laughed, he released her foot and resumed eating.

What exactly did he have planned? Hannah's eyes darted around the apartment. Why was his bedroom door closed? It had been open the last time she'd been here. Adrenaline pumped through her as she turned her gaze back to him.

The man dripped with sex appeal, but just how kinky was he? Had he been putting on a show about not wanting to use the handcuffs? Maybe he had some kind of weird fetish. Just what had she gotten herself into?

"Relax, Hannah; I'm not a freak." Mason's fork clanked on his plate as he pushed away from the table.

"I didn't say a word." She looked up at him as he moved their plates into the sink.

"You didn't have to. You were doing that thing with your eyes. I usually like it, but this time blue was definitely winning."

She narrowed her gaze at him. "What is that supposed to mean?"

He stepped to stand in front of her. "You're having second thoughts."

She was; she really was. But this new position gave her a whole new plan. She could have his jeans around his ankles in fifteen seconds. What man said no to oral sex?

Mason grabbed her hands and jerked her up, plastering her body against his. "Wait!" she yelped. "Aren't we going to have dessert first?"

Mason's laugh was wicked and slow. "Honey, you are dessert."

He was a freak. She knew it now. He was in there preparing for who knew what kind of kinky game. She paced outside his bedroom door and wondered just what she was willing to do about it. Surely not *anything*.

But how could he know? How could he know she'd pushed her own sexual envelope further in the last week with him than she had in her entire life? She simply wasn't prepared for his kind of *anything*.

"Mason?" She hated the way her voice squeaked when she was nervous. "I think I've—"

He swung the bedroom door open, the air from the room rushing over her as she peeked inside. The room was bathed in soft candlelight, dozens of tiny flames flickering against the walls. It looked beautiful, not at all scary.

"You were about to chicken out." It wasn't even a question, and there was no point in denying it.

He took her hand, leading her into the bedroom slowly. His room was much bigger than hers. The wood floors were the same but he had space for a desk and chair. A large mattress and heavy mission-style bed frame dominated the room. He'd pulled down the hunter-green comforter so she saw the navy flannel sheets and pillowcases. Still holding her hand, he neared the bed. Hannah noticed a pillow in the middle of the bed and gasped as she recognized what was on top of it.

"But that's…" Hannah motioned to the electric phallus she knew had fresh batteries.

"Yours? I know. I took it from your nightstand."

Metal glinted in the candlelight. "And those are the handcuffs."

"Turnabout is fair play. And you did say anything."

She had. But did she really mean it? What did he have planned? Her stomach clenched. "Mason, I don't think I can." She sat down on the bed, her back to the pillow. She closed her eyes as the mattress sagged beside her.

He tucked her hair behind her ear and asked, "What can't you do?"

Visions flashed through her mind of all the variations. Thrilled, tantalized, terrified. She swallowed hard. His hands cupped her face, turning her to him. His lips brushed against hers and she breathed deep, inhaling the scent of him, of the room. Jasmine-scented candles? How did he always know what she liked without having to be told?

She parted her lips, inviting him inside so she could feast on all he had in store. She moaned as the kiss deepened, stirring the passion within her. Moving her hands to his chest, she encountered his sweater. "One of us has entirely too many clothes on."

Mason's hand drifted over her shoulder until he was palming her breast. "Not you," he said with a squeeze.

He released her and pulled the sweater over his head. His laugh sounded almost sinister to her as he stood beside the bed and peeled off his jeans. He hadn't been wearing underwear.

He swung her legs to the middle of the bed and pounced on top of her. Hannah closed her eyes tight. In this position she was right next to the pillow. Just what was he planning on doing with the handcuffs, her vibrator? Or was he hoping she'd be doing something to him? She shuddered at the thrill and the uncertainty.

"Are you cold?" he asked, lowering his naked body over hers.

Cold? No. About to spontaneously combust at the sensation? Absolutely. She shook her head as he kissed her neck and stretched her arms up. She relaxed against him until she realized he might be intending to keep them there.

"Mason," she pleaded, trying to free herself from his grasp, but it only made him grab her tighter. Her breath quickened as she looked into his eyes. "You have to tell me what you're going to do."

"I do?" He ducked his head and traced a line from her collarbone to her ear with the tip of his tongue that had her arching off the bed.

"Please." She wanted to know so she could give herself over to the sensations he doused her with.

She heard the handcuffs clink around her wrists before the cool metal locked her hands above her head, anchoring her to his bed frame.

"Much better." He silenced her protests with his mouth, kneading her breasts in his hands.

His kiss was soft and gentle, like his touch. She'd gladly let him touch her like this all night. "You don't need the cuffs, Mason. I'm yours for whatever you need."

He kissed a path from her mouth, down her chin to her neck. He flattened his tongue against her nipple. As he spoke his breath tickled her damp, sensitive flesh. "I need for you to not rush me."

He sucked her nipple deep in his mouth. The connection went all the way to her core, causing her to arch off the bed. He released her and wrapped his fingers around hers, molding her hands against the rail he'd attached her to. "Hold onto this or you'll hurt your wrists."

"I can hold onto it without the cuffs."

"Methinks the lady doth protest too much." Mason's attentions were on her breasts again. This time he rolled her nipples between his fingers, leaned down and let the rough stubble of his cheek make her writhe.

She had to have him. Now. She wrapped her legs around his body and pulled him down on top of her. Shifting her hips, she almost had him.

He cursed and pulled up, both hands pressing her hips into the mattress. The gleam in his eye told her he wanted it as bad as she did. "I told you not to rush me."

"I need you inside of me. Now."

"Me?" He breathed against her ear, still careful to hold her down.

"Yes, you. BOB hasn't done a thing for me since the first time we were together."

He reared back. "Bob?"

"Battery Operated Boyfriend, Mason." She wiggled, but his hands held her tight. "You get so jealous. I'm surprised you'd be willing to share even with my vibrator."

His head hung down. She felt his eyes drinking in her body. "I'm not sharing you with anything."

"Then why did you bring it?"

"I told you, it's more of a show than a tell."

"Then show me."

"Not yet." He released her hips but moved to the side before she clutched him with her legs again. His tongue danced across her body, laving her breasts, tickling her ribs, circling her belly button. He crawled between her legs as he went lower, and placed an open-mouthed kiss on her navel, fanning sensations throughout her body. She gripped the bed frame tighter as he spread her legs, resting them on his shoulders. He took each of her outer lips in his mouth and sucked.

He somehow communicated with her responses on a level even she was unaware of. His fingers spread her open and his tongue plunged inside. She tried to move but he had her anchored below, the handcuffs from above. There was nowhere to go, nothing to do but surrender to his ministrations. A surrender she'd never known, never considered. But what it all meant she'd sort out later.

His mouth did things to her she had never thought possible. She stopped trying to even pay attention to what he was doing and just gave herself over to the feeling. Whether he was using his tongue, his teeth, his fingers, or his breath, she didn't care as long as he didn't stop. Trapped as she was there was no way to even encourage him except with her voice, but the sounds she heard couldn't be coming from her.

Her whole body tensed as the release began, relaxing her in waves from head to toe. Waves crashing against a rocky shoreline, building and breaking, releasing in a smooth foam melting into the sand.

From somewhere she came back down, realizing he'd stopped at some point. She focused on her breathing, trying to bring her heart rate under control so she could hear something over the pounding in her ears.

His fingers pried hers from the bed frame. He was going to release her. Wonderful. She'd thank him in a minute, once she'd caught her breath and found enough energy to open her eyes.

His hands skimmed her body, every inch of her sensitized to his touch. Finally she could move, pressing herself into his talented hands. Except her hands were still bound. She opened her eyes. "Mason?"

The ceiling spun as his hands rolled her over as if she were a rag doll. Quickly he lifted her hips and placed a pillow beneath her. She stared at her fingers as she again grasped the bed frame. She swallowed hard, her throat dry from panting. His hands skimmed up her legs, kneading her buttocks. She squeezed her eyes tight as her stomach clenched. Was this what he meant by *anything*?

His hands spread her legs and the mattress sank where he knelt between them. His fingers slipped down her swollen slit, making her moan and open herself to him more. She heard a familiar hum and the gears started turning in her brain. She thrashed her head from side to side and gripped the bed frame tighter. "No, Mason, I want you, just you. Please. Just you."

Mason lowered his body on hers, pressing her deeper into the mattress. It robbed her of breath before he lifted himself up, holding his weight off of her. "You'll have me." His mouth massaged the tension from her neck, his tongue sending shivers down her spine. The tip of the vibrator slid beneath her, not entering, but pulsing insistently against her clit. She sucked in a breath, overcome by the sensation while she was still so sensitive.

Mason placed an openmouthed kiss on the base of her neck, massaging deeper and deeper. His hands pulled her hips upwards, opening her further to him. He slid inside in one long, smooth motion. Breathing was impossible in the presence of so many wonderful sensations. She trusted her heart to remember to beat. Something about the slow rhythm he set helped her begin to take in air. He pulled out slowly, then thrust into her, filling her to the hilt every time.

The fullness of him and the vibrations from below sandwiched her between two very different kinds of pleasure. It was just too much. Too many sensations coming at her from everywhere. Tension building from so many directions. It couldn't possibly release when it was overwhelming her.

She tried to talk, tried to tell him it was too much, but even sound eluded her. It was all she could do to keep her head above water as the waves hit, crashing against her body from every direction. Her entire body clenched and released with her climax, his rhythm drawing it out longer and longer. Maybe it was possible to die this way. She couldn't move, couldn't speak, and could barely hear primal, feral sounds dying away in the background. And still her body clenched and released, tightened and opened. Continued until all she knew was her own breath.

CHAPTER TWELVE

IT MUST be morning, thought Hannah as she slowly opened her eyes. The room was darkened. Drapes. He must have drapes. She peeked one eye at the alarm clock on the bedside table. Two-thirty? He obviously didn't know how to set a clock.

She opened the other eye. Water. Thank heaven for small favors. She'd never been so thirsty in all her life. She tried to sit up but was stopped by the cuff around one wrist and the throbbing between her legs. Pressing the button on the cuff, she freed herself, and shook her head. "Very funny, Mason." Where was he anyway?

She gingerly sat up, careful not to move her legs too much. The water was gone in two gulps. More, she needed more. And some clothes. She looked down at her bare body. She'd never slept nude in her life.

She scanned the room for something to throw on, but it was clean. He'd even removed the candles burning last night. Carefully she twisted her body so her legs fell off the bed.

As her feet touched the bare floor she heard papers shuffling in the other room. He was still here. And letting her sleep, which was nice, though she'd have rather woken up with him. She tiptoed to the closet, opening it slowly so as not to make any noise.

"You finally up, sleeping beauty?" What was with his hearing?

"I'm awake." Her throat was scratchy, her voice throatier than usual. She snagged a T-shirt off a hanger and pulled it over her head.

"Feel better?" he asked from the doorway. The man even made sweatpants look sexy as he stretched his arms over his head, hooking his fingers in the doorjamb. Even with the ache between her legs, she stepped to him and ran her fingers up the muscles she'd yearned to touch last night.

"Hungry?" he asked. The twinkle in his eye made her wonder exactly what he had in mind for the morning.

She nodded, hoping her body was up to playing games with him.

Taking her hand, he tugged her into the kitchen, pulling out a chair and opening the fridge. She noticed the clock on the microwave behind him. Two thirty-five. She hadn't noticed they were so off last night. "What's with your clocks?"

"My clocks?" He set an egg carton and some cheese on the counter. "Do you want breakfast or lunch?"

"Breakfast." She motioned to the microwave. "It says it's two-thirty."

"Hannah, it *is* two-thirty." He cracked some eggs into a bowl.

Her heart stalled in her chest. She hadn't slept past ten since college. "What?"

Mason shrugged and started beating the eggs. "You were tired."

"I don't sleep until two in the afternoon. Even when I take a sleeping pill. You didn't slip me something, did you?"

"Incredible." He grabbed a pan from the pot rack over the sink and turned to the stove.

Her breath quickened. "Did you?"

Mason chuckled, swirling butter in the pan. "Honey, I didn't slip you anything you didn't ask for."

Hannah crossed her arms across her chest. "I didn't ask to be drugged."

Eggs sizzled in the pan as he turned and looked down at her. "Now I'm starting to get annoyed. Do you feel drugged?"

"No." A little sore and thirsty, and really hungry now that the aroma of the eggs hit the air, but not drugged or hung over.

He pinned her to the chair with his gaze. "Do you honestly think I would drug you?"

"No." He turned his attention back to her breakfast. She felt the color rising from her shoulders to her hairline. She smoothed the tangled mop with her hand, disappointed in herself for even thinking such things.

Mason busied himself making tea, pouring juice, anything but looking at her.

"I'm sorry. I didn't mean—I don't think—oh, hell. I'm just sorry, okay?"

He nodded, still seemingly mesmerized by his culinary abilities.

With a sigh Hannah got up and walked to the bathroom. She must be a ratty-haired, raccoon-eyed mess. She flipped on the light and closed the door, and was stunned by her reflection.

She threw open the door and charged at him. "You washed my face!"

Mason backed against the counter and laughed. "You're welcome?"

She stood on her toes, trying to look him in the eye. "When did you do that? How did you do that?"

He set his hands on her shoulders. "Last night, with a washcloth." He sat her down in the chair and knelt beside her. "You're really bad at the morning after. I mean it, really bad."

His laugh irritated her more. "How did you wash my face without waking me up? I'm a very light sleeper."

"You were pretty wrung out. I didn't know if that stuff would hurt your eyes so I wiped it off. Again, you're welcome." He got up and took the plate from the counter, setting it in front of her.

"What exactly did you do to me last night?"

He folded into the chair across from her. "Do you need diagrams? Because I could do a flow chart that will blow your mind."

"This isn't a joke, Mason. I was just unconscious for the last twelve hours. How am I supposed to feel?"

"Sixteen, and grateful. You were tired."

She rubbed her hands over her face, trying not to picture him gently washing her face as she slept.

When she looked up Mason was across the room thumbing through his bookshelf. Hannah huffed her breath, then drained the juice and started in on the eggs. Pepper jack cheese and roasted red peppers. Nothing about Mason made any sense. He was either the perfect man, or a sociopath.

Completely paranoid. Was she always like this or had the cards and that jackass ex-boyfriend done this to her recently? He pulled the book from the shelf and thumbed through the pages. She'd trusted him so completely last night. It stung she was so skeptical this morning.

Laying the book open on the coffee table, he picked up the magazine he'd been looking at before she'd finally woken up. He'd tried to stay in bed with her this morning so they could wake up together. He had never expected her to be able to sleep this long. He'd had time to clean the apartment and plan out their trip to New Zealand. He might have actually booked the tickets if the computer weren't in the bedroom.

He stared blankly at the picture on the page. People climbed into huge plastic balls and ran down hills. It looked like a good time. Would she think so? "Hannah?" He looked up to find her chair empty.

"What?" she asked, coming out of the bathroom, her fingers busy braiding her hair over her shoulder.

He spun the magazine toward her. "Will you do this?"

Her eyes widened as she grabbed the magazine. Her eyes grew even wider as she sat next to him on the couch. "What are they doing? Why would someone want to run around in a giant hamster ball?"

Mason shrugged. "You'll have to watch me, I guess. I have some other ideas." He lifted another magazine from the stack. "This is where they filmed *Lord of the Rings*. Did you like those movies?"

Hannah shook her head. "Never saw them. I don't have much time for movies." She waved her hand across the stack of magazines. "What's this about?"

"While you were sleeping I went through my magazines and found all the articles about New Zealand. I found some articles on beach resorts. You pick where we stay and I'll plan what we do."

Her body turned toward him. "Do you travel a lot?"

"Three or four times a year. I've wanted to do New Zealand for a while, though. Do you like to travel?"

"I don't know. I've never done it. It's a little frivolous, all that money just for one week."

Mason shrugged. You got what you paid for. "We have to go for at least two. And I'll pay for it."

"You'll take me to New Zealand for two weeks. Just like that?"

Not really, but after this morning he wasn't about to tell her what strings were attached. "You'll love it; I'll make sure." He kissed her on the cheek and grabbed for another magazine. She'd never bungee jump.

"Have you done that?" Her hand splayed across the picture of a woman diving from a bridge, only her ankles tethered. The rebound would be amazing.

Mason nodded. "Four times. Will you?"

"Jump off a perfectly good bridge? Not in this lifetime." She turned to look at him. "Are you an adrenaline junkie?"

Direct, to the point. Deserved the same. "Yes. But I'm not obsessed by it. We can stay at a spa and experiment with just how long you can stay asleep, if that's what you want."

"I don't know what I want," she huffed, reaching for a magazine herself, but coming up with the book. She gasped and pulled it to her chest. "This is what you did last night."

"Yes, but that's not why it's open there. There's a blurb on the bottom about how multiple orgasms might cause you to pass out. It's what I was going for, but I never thought you'd be out all day."

"That's what you were going for?" Her head buried in the book and she began to flip the pages. "My multiple orgasms was your *anything*?"

"No, I wanted you to sleep here. *That* was my *anything*."

She looked up at him slowly. "I would have done that."

He watched her eyes move back and forth. She was trying to decide if she really would have. "You weren't planning to."

She cast her eyes back at the book, and she flipped it around, the naked bodies flashing before him. "I thought you were going to do *this*."

"Why would I do that?" He closed the book and placed it on the table. "If that's your thing we'll try it, but it's not mine."

She tucked her legs beneath her, her breasts hidden beneath the fabric of his T-shirt. "You expect me to believe you just wanted me to sleep?"

"I wanted you to sleep here." He walked his fingers up her bare leg to where the hem of his shirt rested on her thigh. "I sleep better with you." Her eyes narrowed and he actually felt her weighing his words. He closed his eyes and shook his head. He couldn't win with her. "I want you to stay here, with me." He rubbed his fingers back and forth across her thigh, waiting for her protests.

"I only live downstairs, Mason. You seem to be able to hear everything I do anyway. Besides, I'm going to be at work nonstop for the next week. I'll be too tired for anything."

"I'm not asking you to make love with me every night. Just sleep here."

"Is this about the cards? Because there haven't been any more."

"That's a small part of it. Just stay up here until Kate comes home."

Hannah rolled her eyes. "I should stay here when Kate comes home. She and Derek will want some time with their penguins."

He met her smile. This was good; she was at least considering it.

"I'll be at work a lot too. You can use any free time to look around and get to know more about me."

Hannah pulled back. "You want me to snoop? I'm not a snoop."

She had to be kidding. "Hannah, you took my mail on our first date."

She liked it here. The whole place smelled like him, the fridge was full, and occasionally the bed was already warm when she got into it at night.

Her apartment always felt like Kate's place, and even though this was Mason's it felt like home. Relaxing and unpretentious in a way her family home never had been. Hannah reminded herself to be careful as she unzipped her boots and made her way to the bathroom. A girl could get used to this.

He wouldn't be home tonight. She'd learned what he meant about the job scaring her. A few days ago he'd snuck into bed thinking she was already asleep. He'd taken a shower to try to hide the day, but she'd still smelled the smoke in his hair.

He'd played it off as if it were a joke. But in her mind it looked like a made-for-television five-alarm blaze. Making love to him that night had felt like the most natural thing in the world. Slow and simple and completely terrifying. He'd fallen asleep holding her almost immediately after. She'd held onto him all night, wondering if he'd felt the change. She couldn't even pretend she was just having sex with him anymore.

She was falling for him. A long fall that would have her crashing at the bottom when he tired of their sexual one-upmanship. Which he was still winning. She needed an edge.

Hannah surveyed the bookshelf. Where was that sex manual? If she found a dog-eared page she'd finally have an edge over him.

Books for work and the ones he was using to study for his exam lined the top shelf. Hardback best-sellers were next; the paperbacks he read were in his nightstand. Political thrillers he'd called them when she'd come home and found him reading in bed. Photo albums on the third shelf, and a bunch of magazines on the bottom. With the sex manual on top. Finally.

Stooping down to pick up the book, she paused. Had he just been teasing her about snooping, or did he really want her to? She ran her fingers across the mismatched photo albums. If a picture was worth a thousand words...

It would certainly serve him right. She hadn't looked

through his things at all in the time she'd been staying here. Usually she walked through the door, washed her face and was asleep within ten minutes.

But tomorrow was Thanksgiving, so she could sleep in. She wasn't expected at Molly's until lunchtime, wouldn't see Mason until he met her there at eight to go to his parents' house together. Her stomach knotted at the thought. Sleep would be hard to come by tonight.

She'd look through the pictures to make sure nothing surprised her tomorrow. Look out for a two-headed aunt or something. Maybe see if she could find out where he got those eyes.

She curled up on the couch with an album of travel photos. He'd been almost everywhere. And from the looks of it, with quite a few women. It didn't surprise her, but it stung. One day she'd wind up as nothing more than a snapshot tucked into an album.

With a sigh she rose, grabbing the last two albums before sinking back on the couch. Fire training dominated another album. He'd told her he'd fought forest fires during the summers in college, but the pictures made it all too real. She slammed the album shut halfway through. She'd have to look at that one some day when he wasn't at work.

An eight-by-ten of a beautiful brown-eyed baby girl stared out from the front page of the final album. Hannah smiled, immediately recognizing Ryan's nose. This must be Riana. Sure enough the following pages were a testament to the McNally family devotion to the next generation. Anyone holding Riana in the snapshots was smiling. There was one of Derek holding her at arm's length because she was covered in spaghetti; Ryan with his face and her hands covered in finger paint; Mike having a tea party wearing a tiara, and an older woman who must be their mother brushing Riana's long blonde hair. A child would be so blessed to be part of this family.

As she turned the page her breath caught in her throat. Mason was asleep in a recliner with a napping Riana curled up on his chest. He'd be a wonderful father. She slammed her eyes shut at the notion, hot tears prickling her eyelids. She just had baby on the brain because of turning thirty next week. That was all.

She nearly leapt out of her skin as the phone rang. Setting the albums on the coffee-table, she wondered about answering it. It might cause more questions than she was willing to answer if it was his mother or an ex-girlfriend. She picked up the extension. Let an ex-girlfriend know someone was home.

"Good, you're home. I didn't wake you, did I?" Mason's voice rang across the line.

She shook her head as she wiped the moisture from her eyes, and then remembered he couldn't see her. "No, I just got in."

"I'll be quick so you can get to sleep. I might be a little late getting out to your sister's house. They need a few extra hands serving at the mission and since it's only a block away we're going to pitch in. Is that okay?"

Hannah shook her head. Amazing. "You're asking me if it is okay for you to serve Thanksgiving dinner to homeless people?"

His laughter made her smile. "No, I'm asking you to understand if I'm late."

"I think it's wonderful."

"Okay, then."

Hannah settled against the couch cushions and looked down at her nightgown. If he were only here. "Mason? Did you ever watch *Sex and the City*?"

"Not really my thing. Why?"

"One of the characters had a fling with a firefighter, and she came down for a visit one night. They had sex right there against the front of the truck."

"Hannah…" His voice was gravelly and threatening, just the reaction she was hoping for.

"An alarm went off and the entire crew walked in on them."

"I was just starting to be able to sleep here again without embarrassing myself."

"Now we can't have that."

The wail in the background made her stomach clench. "I'll be fine, honey. I've got to go."

The dial tone echoed against her ear as she hung up the receiver. She needed to get used to this. She had told him she'd be okay with it. She needed to be okay with it. He was very smart, and strong, and he swore he was always careful.

She busied herself with shelving the photo albums. Her eyes held on the top shelf. He knew as much about fire as she knew about retail. He'd be okay.

The phone rang again, grating what was left of her nerves. "Hello?"

"It was a false alarm. I'll probably be up all night losing at Scrabble. Get some sleep."

CHAPTER THIRTEEN

"WE'RE all worried about you." Hannah almost lost her dinner as her father cornered her while she looked out the front window.

Hannah turned from the view of an escape. "There's nothing to worry about, Daddy. Marty moved to Maryland. He really is out of my life this time."

Her father's eyes narrowed. "We're not worried about Marty."

"Okay," Hannah said slowly, not at all liking the way this conversation was going.

"This young man you've been keeping company with, Hannah. You need to stop encouraging him."

Her blood began to boil. "Let me get this straight. You're not worried about the man who came after me with a broken bottle in a dark parking lot, but you are worried about Mason. The guy who kept Marty from raping me."

"Don't get hysterical. We're all glad he was there that night, but why was he there, Hannah? Because he's stalking you."

Hannah rolled her eyes. "He's not stalking me, Dad. That's all in Troy's imagination. Mason's actually really wonderful." Hannah hoped he bought the smile she forced.

"You know you aren't the best judge of character. You thought Dalton was an underachiever and he just sold his second novel. You thought Marty was promising, and, well, look at how that turned out."

How was she supposed to argue with that? Her college boyfriend had turned out to have a hidden talent and her last boyfriend had turned out to be a married attacker. "Mason is different. You'll see when you meet him tonight." Her argument held no water, even with her.

Her father shook his head and swirled his brandy. "You need to be more careful. We don't want to see you go through another crisis. We just want you to be happy, get married, start a family. Your priorities are in all the wrong places. You need to be looking for someone more suitable."

She did not want to know what her parents considered suitable. "Dad, I'm very happy with my life." And she was, especially lately.

"You don't want to be married, have children?"

Did she ever. "Maybe some day, but you have to work for those things. They don't just fall into your lap."

"And you can't work for them if you're always at work."

"I'm not discussing my promotion." She turned back to the window and glanced at her watch. *Of all the nights to be late, why tonight?*

"Here you two are." Molly's voice rang across the room. "Come into the family room; we have an announcement to make."

Hannah was grateful for the save. Another minute with her father and he might have found out what hysterical looked like. Why was nothing she did ever good enough?

She looked around the family room at the reason why. Perfection surrounded her. Her older sister Beth sat with her two boys, both wearing white-button down shirts and ties that were still clean. Beth's husband poured sparkling cider and passed the flutes around. Troy held Molly close to him as if she were a doll that might break at any moment. Even her parents looked perfect standing shoulder to shoulder in their holiday best.

She was alone, just as she'd been growing up. Always alone in the middle of a crowded room. Her father tilted his head and whispered a secret to Beth. Her mother reached out and squeezed Molly's hand. Wasn't she supposed to have gotten over this by now?

Sometimes she deluded herself into thinking she had. But then there were moments like this when she saw the emptiness clearly. She wanted Mason here tonight to prove she wasn't alone any more. That someone cared about her. They didn't need to know he was with her because of the sex. She just wanted him to be there so for one moment she wouldn't be so lonely in the middle of them.

Troy cleared his throat, pulling her from her pity party. Molly was smiling so brightly Hannah couldn't help but smile back. She didn't want her sisters to be any less happy. She just wanted some of that fullness for herself. She shook the cobwebs from her head. Turning thirty was turning her into a sap.

"We're glad everyone could be here tonight. We have an announcement, and we wanted to tell everyone together." Troy looked down lovingly at Molly. He could be a nice guy when he wasn't nosing into Hannah's business.

Molly turned to the group. "We're having a baby!"

Beth was so excited she nearly knocked her youngest to the ground. *A baby*.

Hannah rose and hugged her sister. "I knew you couldn't like chili that much." She stepped back so her mother could rub Molly's nonexistent belly.

The sparkling cider was gone in one long gulp. Hannah looked at her excited family. This would make a much better impression on Mason. They could all talk about the impending arrival instead of whether or not he was stalking her.

"When are you quitting?" Hannah froze as her mother's words hung in the air.

"Why would she quit?" she heard her voice say before she bothered with eye contact.

"Because, Hannah, she's going to have a baby. Family is more important than a simple job."

"Molly doesn't have a job, Mother, she has a successful career. She is very good at what she does and there is no reason she can't continue to work and be a mother."

"She'll want to be with her baby."

Molly broke into the conversation. "*She* is in the room. This is a conversation for another time."

Hannah stared her mother down. She wouldn't guilt Molly to give up her career. Rage boiled inside of her, her blood already on simmer from her conversation with her father. They would not pressure Molly too.

Her mother broke the gaze first. "If you're going back to work we're moving back. Someone has to take care of this baby."

"Mom, that's not necessary," Molly said, looking at Hannah. "I'm planning to work until I'm due in May. Then I'll take a couple of years off."

Hannah marched from the room and up the stairs. She tried to make out the emotion choking her. Disappointment, jealousy, pride? She couldn't quite tell. But whatever it was, it made her sick.

Even the frantic folding and hanging of her laundry couldn't calm her. Nothing short of a screaming match with her parents could unload this much resentment and anger. Hannah knew she was smart, and hardworking, and good enough, damn it. Why did they always make her feel as if she'd never measure up?

They knew enough to stay out of her way as she made

three trips to get all the laundry into Kate's car. Mason finally arrived as she carried the last of it out of the house.

"I have to get out of here. Now." Hannah shoved a basket of laundry into Kate's car and turned to face him.

He was only ten minutes late. "Shouldn't you be putting this stuff in the truck?"

"What? Why?" She spat the words so harshly Mason took a step back.

He exhaled slowly. "Because you're dropping the car off for Kate at my folks' house."

Hannah looked up at the night sky. "This day just keeps getting better and better."

He unlocked the back door of the Bronco and placed the laundry basket on the seat, doing the same with an armload of clothes on hangers and another basket. His laundry basket. She'd done his laundry?

When he closed the door Hannah was waiting for him. She wrapped her arms around his waist and looked up at him. "I will do anything you want, anything for a week, if you don't make me go tonight."

What the hell had happened here? He wrapped his arms around her, tucking her head beneath his chin. He hated when she felt this way. Hated when she tried to barter sex for understanding. Hated that she thought she had to.

"We'll be fast at my folks'. Just drop Kate the keys and we'll be gone."

Hannah shook her head and looked at the ground. "I'm being such a baby." Her whisper was barely audible as she pulled away and wiped her eyes. They had made her cry? What was wrong with these people?

He tilted her chin to look him in the eye. "What happened?"

She lowered her lashes. He felt her taking deep breaths, trying to calm herself.

He stepped closer, his body pressing against hers. "It's just us out here; you don't have to put on a brave face."

She dropped her shoulders, but didn't look up. "You want the good news or the bad news?"

He rubbed her arms. "Both."

She lifted her chin, a slight grin playing on her lips. "My baby sister is pregnant."

Mason gave a slow smile. "That must be the good news."

"Yeah." She sniffed. "She's quitting her job."

Mason shrugged. "Some women do, especially when their kids are babies." Hannah tried to pull away, but he held her firm. That had to be what this was about. "I don't expect you to."

She shrugged him off and stepped away. "Mason, we haven't even been dating a month."

Hearing the front door open, they both turned and watched Troy approach. With a sideways glance at Mason, he turned to Hannah. "I'm not going to let you take this from her. She's been worried about your reaction for months. You go back in there and fake it if you have to."

Who did this clown think he was? Mason's fists balled at his sides. "Don't tell her what to do."

Hannah stepped closer to him, wrapping her fingers over his clenched fist. "We were just about to make our goodbyes."

Troy narrowed his gaze at Mason. "Don't say hello and you won't need a goodbye."

"He does, or I don't," Hannah said before he could speak.

Troy threw his hands in the air and marched back into the house.

Mason turned back to Hannah. "What's his problem?"

"He still thinks you're dropping the cards to scare me so you can save me." She feigned a whisper.

Mason rolled his eyes. "That's ridiculous."

"I know. But I can't exactly tell him how I know the cards

aren't from you without getting too graphic." Her eyes danced with meaning.

Mason smiled. He was having the same problem convincing his father Hannah wasn't dropping the cards herself.

"You don't have to go in there if you don't want to. I won't blame you, knowing what they think you're doing."

Mason pulled her toward the door. "They better get used to me." Swinging her arm, he toyed with the box in his pocket. This night would not be going as planned.

"You're really very charming." Hannah slammed the car door to punctuate her statement. Walking to the Bronco, she stood next to him in his parents' driveway, tossing her bag through the open driver's side door.

"Why do you sound surprised?" Mason shut his door with a grin.

"Charming me out of my panties is one thing, but you wrapped my mother around your little finger in less than a minute." She'd never seen anyone disarm her mother so fast. And her father had actually shaken his hand when they'd left. It was nothing short of miraculous.

He reached for her hand, pulling it between them and playing with her fingers. "I'm glad you're in a better mood."

"Me too." She let out a long sigh. "I'm nervous."

"Me too." He laughed.

Hannah rolled her eyes. "They're your family. What do you have to be nervous about?"

He shrugged his shoulders. "I've never done this before."

Why did she never know what he meant? "This? What are we going to do?"

A slow smile lifted the corners of his mouth. "I've never brought someone home for a holiday."

"What? Why not?" Even she'd done that. Once.

He leaned back against the truck and pulled her to him. "I only just found you."

Her expression softened. "That's a wonderful line, but can you be serious for a minute? What about all the women you took on trips?"

She felt his body rise and fall as he laughed. "All what women?"

As if this were funny. "The women in your pictures."

He pressed his forehead against hers. "Oh, so you did snoop. I wondered what you'd find."

She pouted at having given herself away. "Are you going to tease me or answer my question?"

His grip tightened, pulling her up on her toes. "You've really never traveled, have you?"

She shook her head, realizing at some point he'd pinned her arms to her sides.

"When you travel you meet people and take pictures so you'll remember them. I've never taken a woman on vacation before."

She wiggled against his grasp. "You're freaking me out here." And not from being trapped against him.

"Mason, I thought I heard you out here." A beautiful older woman scurried out of the garage, her arms laden with Tupperware. Hannah recognized Mason's mother from the photos. Mason must have inherited her hearing because they had barely been speaking above a whisper.

"Happy Thanksgiving, Mama." Mason only squeezed Hannah tighter, lifting her completely off the ground. Fantastic first impression. He had to be telling the truth. He obviously hadn't done this before.

"I saved you some of everything, but I don't want your brothers to see." She rounded the truck and peered at the laundry in the back seat.

"I'm her favorite," Mason whispered loud enough for the world to hear. Finally he put Hannah down. "Let's hide it in the back. I brought a cooler."

Hannah stepped back, glad her feet were once again firmly on the ground. She watched the quiet interaction of mother and son as they packed the morsels away.

As if he sensed how starved for affection she felt, Mason moved to her side and wrapped an arm around her shoulder. "Hannah, this is my mother, Mary Jean."

The older woman's cinnamon-brown eyes warmed over her as she leaned in for an embrace. Her stomach fluttered as she felt the soft lips against her cheek. "We're so glad you're with us tonight, Hannah. We've all been dying to meet the woman captivating Mason."

When she pulled away her smile was wide and genuine. Not at all monster-in-law. Hannah tried to force a smile, only to realize her cheeks had already complied.

"Come on inside, you two. I'm sure Kate will be glad to see a familiar face. I'm afraid the boys haven't given her a moment to herself since she arrived."

Mason took her hand, swinging it between them as they followed his mother into the house. The sound of boisterous laughter hit her harder than the warm air rushing out of the door. She felt swept away by the whirlwind of introductions, thankful when Kate finally grabbed her hand and pulled her down on a patterned sofa.

"I'm so glad you're here. If I have to tell one more person where I went to college, I'm going to scream."

Kate was positively glowing. Maybe she *was* in love with Derek.

"How was Vegas?"

Kate grabbed for her wineglass from the coffee table and drained it in one swallow. "Have you seen Derek?"

Hannah shook her head. Derek was the only McNally she hadn't seen in the last five minutes.

"I need to find him. Honey, I will be right back." Kate got up, leaving Hannah alone on the couch in a crowd of people she didn't know. She crossed her legs and placed her folded hands on her lap. She wished Mason had told her to change. Everyone wore jeans and sweaters, while she was still wearing the dress from the more formal Thanksgiving meal with her family.

As he slid next to her on the sofa she realized why. He hadn't thought to change from his work clothes. He looked exactly as he had the first time she'd laid eyes on him.

Mason flashed her a smile. "So what do you think?"

She had no idea what to make of anything when he smiled at her that way. "They all have brown eyes," she whispered in his ear.

"Very observant, Miss Daniels." He pulled her away from the couch and up the stairs.

If he thought he was pulling her upstairs for a quickie he had another think coming. "Where are we going?" she asked, running into the back of him when he stopped short.

He stepped behind her, directing her attention to the collage of pictures on the wall. "There he is." His finger tapped a framed snapshot of an elderly man sitting on the floor playing Lincoln logs with a tow-headed toddler. "Francis Mason, meet Hannah Daniels." Hannah leaned closer. The old man's eyes were definitely blue, but she'd never know if they were the same blue.

"You have his eyes?" she asked, turning to face him.

"So I've been told." He backed down a step and looked her in the eye. "Would you look at that?"

"What?" she asked, not caring the answer. His eyes were almost hypnotic the way they rolled across her face.

"When I'm down here we're exactly the same height." Her gaze focused on his mouth. She suddenly realized she hadn't kissed him in three days. Not since Monday night. Where had the time gone?

But she couldn't kiss him here, now. She settled for tracing his lips with her fingertip, her stomach clenching as he leaned in. Maybe it wouldn't look so bad if he kissed her.

"Hands where I can see them, Mason. The rules don't change just because you move out." Mac's words were gruff and caused a blush Hannah was sure extended to the roots of her hair, but he smiled as he walked by them.

Mason pulled back. "That man must have radar."

Marry me. The words echoed in his head. It wasn't what he'd planned, and he knew she deserved more than a whisper on his parents' staircase, but he just wanted to get it out. He'd only got the ring yesterday, too afraid she might find it if she went snooping.

Kate had been so helpful, telling him the size and the style Hannah liked. She would like the ring. He wanted to get married the first week she had off and honeymoon in New Zealand for the other two.

Her parents were in town until her birthday, a week from now. There'd be time to clear it with her folks later. First he needed to convince her to trust herself, him, and them.

"Hannah?"

"Everybody, can I have your attention?" Derek jumped on top of the coffee table to address the crowd. "Now that everybody is finally here I have an announcement to make.

"First I want to thank Mason and Hannah for introducing me and Katie." Derek looked down and smiled at the blonde woman looking up at him. "I looked at this woman and thought, Wow. This must be a mercy date."

The family laughed and Mason took Hannah's hand. "Before we even left the bar that night I told her I was in love with her. It was the most amazing night of my life, and then she got on a plane the next morning."

As the crowd sighed Mason noticed Kate was blushing and he squeezed Hannah's hand. "I called her incessantly, harassing her until she agreed to see me again. Last weekend in Las Vegas. Before she changed her mind I talked her into marrying me right then and there."

CHAPTER FOURTEEN

SOFT fingers tugged on Hannah's wrist and pulled her inside the warm kitchen. Hannah looked at Mary Jean, wondering if she thought Derek and Kate's announcement was crazy too. There was worry in her eyes. Did she think Hannah might try a similar stunt with Mason?

"I just wanted to warn you," Mary Jean said in hushed tones. "Mason may have a little trouble with this."

Any sane person would. Hannah nodded. "I completely understand."

"Good." Mary Jean sighed and leaned back against the counter. "I just remember how it affected him when Ryan got married first, and then again when they announced they were having Riana. He was depressed for weeks. Not jealous, mind you, just wondering if it would ever happen for him."

Hannah could only nod.

Mary Jean shook her head and smiled. "We expected something like this from the other boys, but Derek is usually so much more cautious."

Hannah's head bobbed frantically. Nothing tonight was going as she expected. But while she had the McNally matron's attention she could at least put in a few good words about her newest daughter-in-law. "So is Kate. She is very smart; all of her decisions are weighed and measured. I've known her for ten years and she has never done anything so impulsive."

"Really? She seems fun, spontaneous."

A grin played at Hannah's lips. That was Kate. "Spontaneous, yes, but never reckless."

"Reckless?" Mary Jean's voice lilted through the room she ruled.

How to dig herself out of his hole? "Not that Derek isn't fantastic. Kate liked him just from his resume." This was going from bad to worse. "I never imagined she'd put so little forethought into such a big decision. That either of them would. To marry someone you've barely known a week is a huge leap of faith."

Mary Jean let out a sad chuckle and shook her head. "Not really. They have a lifetime to get to know each other." The older woman smiled and met Hannah's gaze. "Hannah, are you in love with Mason?"

"What?" The word escaped her before she had time to think. Hannah scanned the kitchen for a hidden camera. Mary Jean was violating eight different mother-in-law rules with that question.

"Because if you're not, he deserves to know." Mary Jean leveled her gaze. "Now."

So this was the monster-in-law. Hannah should have known the woman was too good to be true. "We haven't been dating long enough for anyone to be discussing love."

"Love is something you feel, not something you think about. If you have to talk yourself into it, then it will never work. No matter how long or hard you think about it. You either love someone, or you don't. It's surprisingly black and white."

"You're awfully quiet," Mason said as they made the drive home in the dark. She hadn't said a word since she'd told him,

"I have to get out of here. Now." For the second time that night. She had kept herself pressed against the passenger door ever since they'd got into the truck, effectively keeping herself out of his reach.

Was she just tired, or was there something more? He couldn't help if he didn't know. "Are you still upset about Molly?"

"Of course not. She'll be an amazing mother and if she doesn't want to go back to work that's her business." From the corner of his eye he noticed she gave the speech to the window.

"You're just worried your parents will expect the same from you?" He tried to fill the silence with reassurance. "Our situation is very different, Hannah. I only have to work twelve days a month. You could work your schedule around that, plus there's my mom."

"Mason." The edge in her voice set his posture straight. "We are not at a point where we need to be having this discussion. Especially tonight."

He gripped the steering wheel until his knuckles were white. That hurt as if she'd just kicked him. He caught glimpses of her staring out the window, her face shadowed from the dashboard lights. This was not even close to the drive home he had imagined when he'd woken up this morning.

Obviously a subject change was in order. "Derek and Kate won't be able to take their honeymoon until after her case wraps up in January. What do you think about them coming with us to New Zealand?"

She rolled her head back against the seat. "They won't want another couple tagging along on their honeymoon. They need all the time alone they can find just to get to know each other. They're practically strangers."

Alarms flashed in his head, warning him to proceed with

caution. "They're in love. That's all they need to know. They'll work the rest out later."

"You cannot possibly be so naive. This is a recipe for disaster. They don't even know if they want the same things." Finally she was turning toward him, and her eyes were flashing brighter than the headlights of the passing cars.

"It's a recipe for success. Derek and Kate have done a lot of talking on the phone. I'm sure they've covered all the deal breakers. And, besides, it worked for my parents."

She reared her head back so quickly he feared she might smack it into the window. "What do you mean it worked for your parents?"

"They got married three days after they met."

He heard her suck in a ragged breath that robbed his lungs of air. "You never told me that before." Her head fell heavily against the seat, and then she pounded it against the headrest three times. "No wonder she turned on me."

Turned on her? "What are you talking about?"

"This proves my point exactly. I made an ass of myself with your mother. I said I thought Kate and Derek were reckless because they hadn't known each other a week. Twice as long as your parents did." She pounded her head a few more times. "That was need-to-know information, Mason. Do yourself a favor and tell your next girlfriend that tidbit."

He took the corner too fast, but he didn't care. Maybe smashing against the door would knock some sense into her. She was trying to be mean and he didn't like it one bit. "Is that why you wanted to leave?"

"I've just had enough of this day." Hannah struggled to right herself as he took another corner, this time knocking her his way. "Everybody has lost their minds, and they're looking at me like *I'm* crazy."

"Your sister is pregnant and your best friend got married. Some people would think this was a good day for you." Mason set his jaw to bite back the rest of the words as he negotiated their way into downtown.

Her whole body shifted in her seat as she rubbed her right arm. "I'm not jealous."

He hadn't even thought of that, until now. He turned and caught her eyes boring into him. Very green. They almost matched.

"And I'm not hormonal about turning thirty either. I'm just being rational about the situations." She plopped back against the seat and stared straight ahead.

So that was how old she was going to be. It had stung when Ryan announced he and Tara were having a baby the month before Mason turned thirty. He'd been thrilled for them, but had wanted the same in his own life. He could only imagine it being worse for a woman. "I understand how you feel. When Ryan had Riana—"

"I know, you were depressed for weeks. Your mother told me."

"She did?" Just what had gone down between them?

"Yes. She was worried you might be upset about the wedding, but you seem way too comfortable with it."

Mason circled their building looking for a parking spot. "Of course I'm comfortable with it. My brother has never been happier."

"He's setting himself up for a fall. What's between them is obviously physical and when that burns out where will they be? Divorce court." She threw her hands in the air. "And Kate swore she'd never get divorced after what happened with her folks. This is going to tear her up."

"You're so cynical." He jerked the Bronco into a parking spot and killed the engine. "They'll make it work." He had to believe that. Derek wasn't any more prepared for a divorce than Kate was.

"I'm a realist. They haven't spent enough time together to learn what bothers them about the other person. You have to know what's wrong with someone before you can decide if you can live with it."

Mason hopped out of the truck, circling around to her side, but she'd already gotten out. Of course. He stacked a laundry basket on top of the cooler. He wanted to tell Hannah to leave the other one, but it was already in her arms, piled with the hanging items. "What's wrong with me?" he asked as they made their way inside.

Hannah trudged up the stairs, seeming to ponder her answer. When they reached her apartment she turned to face him. "You're possessive, and short-tempered."

He was only possessive of her, which triggered the temper he usually kept under control. Mason dropped the laundry basket on the floor. The clothes jumped up, and then neatly fell back into their piles.

"And you're nosy and distrusting and you get mean when you're hurt or scared. I can live with it. Can you?"

Hannah set her basket on the ground and fumbled with her keys. "Not tonight, Mason."

Taking the key from her, he slid it in the lock and pushed the door open. "Can you?"

She spun to face him and ripped the keys from his hand. "Knock it off!" Her eyes were so bright they were throwing sparks. Blue sparks. Not good. "I can take care of myself."

He was not going to rise to the bait. He piled her basket on top of his and carried the entire load into her bedroom. He didn't even jump when she slammed the door. He started to sort through the baskets to pull out what was his, but she'd already done that. As efficient at laundry as she was at everything else.

He propped his basket against his hip and marched to the living room. She wasn't there. "Hannah?" Had she gone upstairs already?

"I'm tired of talking." He spun around to the sound of her voice as she stepped out of the bathroom. His mouth went dry.

She did not fight fair. She wore a red satin nightgown that went all the way to the floor. The red lace trim accented her full breasts and the slit went from the floor to her hip. She even wore the red stilettos from that time with the chair. He swallowed hard. He could control himself. This wasn't over yet.

It was all over. She was not going to discuss marriage or babies one more time tonight. Mason's priorities were severely distorted from the events of the evening. Hannah had been simmering with restless energy all night. They'd burn it off and both feel better.

For some reason Mason held the laundry basket in front of him like a shield. It might have offended her if she couldn't see the desire burning in his eyes. He wanted this as much as she did.

"We need to finish this conversation." His protest might be convincing if his voice hadn't cracked.

Hannah shook her head, her hair falling in front of her shoulders, and began to stalk toward him. She knew what she needed tonight, and it wasn't more crazy talk. She needed to lose herself in the moment. She needed time and work and family and lost chances to fall by the wayside, tangled and forgotten in her insatiable need for him.

"Hannah, no." He took a step back.

"What do you mean, no?" She tried to take the laundry basket from him, but he held it firm. She did not want to be playing games now.

"I'm not going to make love with you so you can get out of talking to me."

She stepped closer. "Then just have sex with me." She leaned in and whispered in his ear, her hot breath puffing the words. "Fast, hard, hot."

He jumped away as she reached for the waistband of his pants, backing all the way to the front door. The lust in his eyes vanished. "What is this about?"

How to explain what she barely understood? She just needed to be with him, to have him inside of her when she came apart, to have him hold her as the pieces fell back into place. Somehow he fed the hunger for love that was so deep in her soul it could never be filled. How could she tell him and not be weak? She couldn't, not tonight when she was barely keeping herself upright.

He hugged the basket closer and exhaled slowly. "Just put on a robe and we'll go home and finish this conversation."

Hannah shook her head. She needed him to stop talking before he started saying things he didn't really mean just to keep up with his brother. She needed to be in control of her responses, even if they were just physical. And she needed a home court advantage tonight.

"I'm home. I live here."

Mason flashed her a smile. "That's one of the things I want to talk about. I want you to move in with me."

Her stomach clenched and she closed her eyes. This had to be what his mother was warning her about. He'd push their relationship ahead so he wouldn't feel left behind.

"Why?" she asked, barely above a whisper.

"I like having you close." He grinned across the room. "Kate is moving in with Derek, so your living situation is changing anyway."

The perfect reason for cohabitation. "It would certainly

make the sex more convenient. No pesky flight of stairs to get in the way."

"Knock it off, Hannah." His smile disappeared and he shifted the basket to his hip. "It's not like that with us and you know it."

"Oh, that's right." She crossed her arms over her chest and wished she'd put on a robe as he'd asked. "You won't have sex with me tonight."

Mason shook his head. "Not tonight or any other. And not until you let me fix what's got you so upset."

Her temperature rose for a whole new reason. "You want to fix me."

Finally he put the basket down. "That's not how I meant it. I don't want you to feel the way you do right now."

She threw her hands in the air. "You're telling me how to feel now? You know what, Mason? I did a pretty good job of taking care of myself before you ever came into my life. I can handle everything without you telling me how to feel."

"Hannah, don't get hysterical." He stepped closer, but this time it was her turn to back away.

It was one thing to reject her physically, but to be the second man tonight to tell her not to get hysterical? No way.

"I'm not hysterical, but I'm rapidly approaching it. All I wanted from you tonight was an orgasm. Something to help me remember where we are, and forget all the craziness."

"Where we are?" He rubbed his neck as he began to pace around the room. "What does that mean?"

Hannah rolled her eyes. That had to be a rhetorical question. Though from his silence she wasn't so sure. "We're sleeping together."

He went pale. "That's what you think is going on?"

"Mason, that's what *is* going on. I haven't deluded myself into thinking there's more to it. We've known each other less than a month. You obviously feel the same, and you want to live together to move things forward. Which I'm not going to do."

His hands ran through his hair, affecting its usual disarray but little. "That's not why I want us to be together." He stepped to her and grabbed her arms. "Hannah, I love you. You know that."

A nervous giggle escaped her. "You love me. Tonight. The night your brother announces he just got married. Of course you're in love with me. You have to keep up."

"I've loved you since the moment I saw you."

The room started to swirl.

"You didn't even know my name." She shrugged it off. If this was his idea of a joke it wasn't funny. "Don't worry, I won't hold you to it. Your mother warned me you'd be upset about Derek getting married."

"I don't care what my mother said, and I'm not upset about Derek and Kate. You are." He tried to touch her again but she pulled back. She couldn't trust herself to be in control of her emotions now that he'd sent her reeling. "I'll admit I was a little jealous, but not the way you think. I'm jealous they both trust what they feel, while you need for us to go slower."

"If you're in such a hurry, go ahead without me." She'd let him off the hook; what more did he want? Complete mortification tomorrow when he realized what he'd said?

He captured her hands, holding them firm as she tried to pull them back. "I love you and I want to be with you, forever. We'll figure it all out. Where we live and babies and when we get married. Whatever you want. I just want to take care of you."

"That's not what I want. I can take care of myself." She yanked her hands away. What she wanted was all too real right now. He admitted he was jealous of his brother; his mother had warned her. She would not let herself buy into his momentary lapse and be devastated later. She would not. No matter how tempting.

Mason's expression fell as he backed away, his eyes not leaving her face. "When you figure out what you do want, you let me know. I'm tired of hitting my head against a wall with you. I'm sick of being punished for things I didn't do." His voice rose with every word, louder and louder until no other sound existed. "I hate that you have to be naked to communicate with me. How much of this do you expect me to take, Hannah? Every time you get scared you rail on me. You're just pushing me away so that you won't risk getting hurt. But it's not going to help. We're already there."

"Stop psychoanalyzing me. I don't want to be told how I feel, what I want." Her eyes were heavy, but she would not let the tears fall. He would not see how badly her soul had been shredded tonight.

"You're killing me here. The things you accuse me of are so off base, and you know it. So if I'm not what you *want*, Hannah, then we're done. No more."

In one swift move he picked up his laundry and was out the door. She stared at the door for a long time, until she was sure she was strong enough not to chase him up the stairs. It was late and she had to work so early tomorrow. She slowly walked back to her bedroom, her heels clicking with every step.

She plopped down on the bed she hadn't slept in for over a week and set her alarm. Though she doubted she'd sleep tonight. It was already too late to take a sleeping pill, her vibrator and romance novels were collecting dust on Mason's nightstand upstairs, and her brain was an echoing chasm of words from tonight. Warnings that would not leave her alone. And yet she was. Alone, with her laundry.

CHAPTER FIFTEEN

"Wake up, old man," Mason said, kicking the slippers sticking out from under the shiny black GTO.

"I'm not asleep." Mac slid out from under the car, clutching a sparkling clean crescent wrench.

"We all know you come out here to get away from Mom and nap. I'm not in the mood to argue." Mason stalked to the fridge and pulled out two beers, handing one to his father once he righted himself.

"I have to go somewhere. Ever since she retired and started taking care of Riana it's nothing but work in there." Mac jerked his thumb toward the house. "You don't have kids so you don't know."

And at this rate he never would. "Dad, they're shopping. No one is in the house."

"But they'll be back." The old man smiled, a lone dimple appearing in his left cheek.

Mason took a long draw from his beer and got down to business. "Did Mom tell you what she said to Hannah?"

Mac took a swallow and reached across his workbench, finding a pot of wax and a rag. "Why don't you ask your mother?"

Mason leaned his elbows on the workbench and watched

his father begin to polish what could only be dust from the fender. "She's not here, and you are. And don't bother telling me to wait for her. I'm asking you."

Mac peered at the paint on the fender as if it held the meaning of life. "MJ doesn't think Hannah knows you very well."

Neither did Hannah, but he disagreed. "Hannah didn't know your marital history, but she obviously knows me better than Mom. What did she say exactly?"

"Hannah won't tell you?" Mac replaced the wax and grabbed a few cotton swabs.

"She won't tell me what Mom said to upset her." Not that he'd asked. And now he couldn't. He had to give her some breathing room, even if it killed him.

"MJ means well, son. She's just worried you're taking things more seriously than Hannah is. She simply said that if Hannah wasn't in love with you she should tell you."

Mason lowered his eyes and shook his head. Hannah barely trusted her instincts as it was; to have them openly challenged must have been a real blow. No wonder she'd been so upset.

"So did she?" Mac asked as he wiped a cotton swab across an immaculate wheel.

"Hannah loves me, Dad; I'm not worried about that." And he wasn't, though he realized for the first time she hadn't said it back, hadn't said it at all.

"So now what?" Mac turned his attention to the headlamp.

Mason shrugged. "Now I wait for her to figure out what she wants."

"This girl of yours sure spooks easy. She'll have to get used to MJ. The woman won't put on kid gloves for anyone."

"She'll be fine once she realizes she can trust herself. I just have to be patient."

Mac turned to look at him and arched an eyebrow. "Can you do that?"

He wasn't so sure. Last night he had wanted to throw her to the floor and illustrate the difference between having sex and making love. Prove his point and move on with the conversation. But one look in her pale eyes and he'd known he had to tread carefully. She needed to choose him for herself even more than he needed to be chosen.

"I'm giving her a week."

He wasn't imagining it. Someone was definitely moving around downstairs in Hannah's apartment. He sat up on the bed and listened closer. At first he'd thought he'd been dreaming, hallucinating a reason to go downstairs and apologize, though he'd meant every word he'd said. But then he'd looked at the clock and realized there was no way she'd be home.

His bare feet slipped onto the floor in silence. He'd changed into sweat pants and a T-shirt when he'd come back from his volunteer shift this morning. Not that his mind had slowed enough for him to sleep.

His breath caught as he heard something again. A door slamming maybe? He checked the clock again. It was only three and the earliest she'd be home was eight, though ten was more likely. And Kate was still in Klamath Falls.

Maybe she was sick, a cold, the flu, or just feeling awful about the ugliness that had gone on between them. He walked to the kitchen and opened a cupboard to grab her jasmine tea and the cocoa mix she liked, but stopped. She needed some reason to come back upstairs.

On his way out the door he spied the tiny black box sitting on a stack of magazines on the coffee-table. His palms were suddenly damp. Hannah might not know what she wanted, but Mason was sure. Maybe if she knew how serious he was about them? He shoved the box in his pocket and tried to pretend he hadn't broken out in a cold sweat as he made his way back downstairs.

He crept out of his apartment and down the stairs. He wished he had a key. Then he could just walk in and surprise Hannah, or the burglar. He rapped softly on the door and listened, but no response came.

What if it wasn't Hannah moving about? He slowly twisted the knob until it caught. Locked. With all the fireproofing tape he'd jammed in the doorframe it would hurt like hell to break it in. Plus, that would really piss her off. He let out an angry huff of breath and settled for spooking the cat burglar out a window. He'd wait for Hannah to come home and scope the place out then.

He beat the door with the side of his fist. "Hannah! Kate!" Maybe it was that jerk of a brother-in-law. "Whoever is in there, open the door!" He'd like to get a few swings at that guy.

He listened as footsteps approached. He thought about covering the peephole with his thumb, but crossed his arms across his chest instead. The door swung open and Mason cringed.

Hannah's father leveled his gaze. "I wish I could say it's nice to see you again, Mason, but given the circumstances I'm sure you'll understand. What are you doing banging on my daughter's door?"

Mason wished he'd spent more time schmoozing her father and less time charming her mother. "I live right upstairs and I heard you moving around. Kate is out of town and Hannah won't be home until at least eight. I thought someone might have broken in."

"You routinely listen to the happenings in Hannah's apartment?"

Mason reminded himself her father had every right to be concerned. "No, sir. I've just been on edge because of the cards and the incident in the parking lot."

The older man narrowed his gaze. "The cards Troy thinks you're sending her."

Mason fought the urge to roll his eyes. "I didn't drop the cards. They upset me more than Hannah, anyway. She's convinced it's just a neighbor playing a prank."

"But you disagree?"

"I don't want to take any chances with Hannah."

"Me either." The older man stepped out of the doorway and motioned Mason inside. "Call me John. I'd offer you something to drink but her fridge is pretty bare."

"That's good. It means she's eating something that doesn't come out of a vending machine. She's almost finished the oranges I left."

Her father watched intently as Mason checked the citrus, tossing a soft one in the garbage. "You don't mind doing her grocery shopping?"

So this was where she got it from. "I like cooking, she likes eating. It works out great."

"Hannah always hated cooking. She was always more interested in my business magazines than her mother's recipe books."

Mason smiled. He could see that. "Hannah told me she used to wake up early just to talk to you about business."

"She remembers that?" The man's face lit up like a Christmas tree. "She was so little. That stopped when she was about ten and I started staying in town during the week." John shook his head. "She was always such a smart girl. I don't know how she got stuck working at a mall."

Mason took a deep breath. Yes, this was definitely where she got it. "She manages a multimillion-dollar department store. It takes a lot of intelligence to juggle all she does. She has to manage the staff, the freight, the merchandising, the sales volume and a million other things I only pretend to understand."

John knit his brows together. "We have reservations at Mon Desir for dinner on Hannah's birthday. You should come."

Mason nodded, unsure what to say. When they'd played twenty questions Hannah had gone on and on about how she hated French food. "Is that French?"

John nodded. "My wife read a write-up in one of her magazines."

Mason bit his lip, then decided to risk it. It was Hannah's birthday after all. "Hannah doesn't like French food. She likes spicy ethnic or comfort food."

The older man raised an eyebrow. "We went to a French restaurant last year for her birthday."

"Did she eat?" Mason was willing to bet a year's salary on the answer. Hannah thought a chef was trying to hide something if he covered food in a heavy sauce or decorated the plate.

John paused, then shook his head. "Actually, she said she wasn't feeling well and Kate took her home early."

Mason nodded, holding the other man's suddenly guilty gaze. "I have an idea of what she'd like, but there is something I need to talk to you about first."

No tea. Hannah slammed the cupboard door with all the strength she could muster after eight hours of sleep in the last three days. She closed tonight, so she didn't have to be at work for another hour and a half. All she wanted was to sit and sip a nice cup of tea before she got ready. And even that was too much to ask.

She plopped her butt on the couch. She knew where her tea was. It was upstairs, in Mason's apartment. She still had a key. He'd given it to her when he'd asked her to stay. And she knew without looking at the schedule he'd left that he wouldn't be off until seven and it was only six.

The entire procedure would probably take all of ninety seconds. She could even leave his key on the counter. The thought sat in her belly like lead. It would be easier to give it back than have him ask for it. But giving it back would be an opportunity to talk to him, to talk him into giving them another shot.

She'd been pushing him away from the moment they'd met; only he had been stronger, pulling her closer each time. Until she had finally pushed so hard he'd had no choice but to let go.

Everything about the way he made her feel terrified her. You were supposed to fall in love slowly, to ease into it. But Mason McNally had hit her full force from the first second. Even when she'd thought he was all wrong.

She hadn't spoken to him since he'd dropped her off on Thanksgiving. They'd both worked the next day, so it was easy to write off the silence. And she had no idea what to say, or do.

He was right; it was much easier to communicate with him when they were naked, when she felt his response. Her eyes felt heavy, full of tears. But she wasn't going to cry about this again. Not when there was still hope. Her birthday was tomorrow. Maybe he'd let her apologize then.

Hannah pushed off the couch and propelled herself into the bathroom. She'd feel better after a shower. She went through her morning routine on autopilot. Shouldering her bag and locking the door, she set off for the coffee shop, focusing on the reward. Piping hot tea and a fresh bagel.

She intended to take her breakfast with her and hop the train to work. Once she was at the store she'd have no time for this self-indulgent pity party. But she recognized the writing group at their perch in the corner and decided to take a seat in the velvet armchair. Five minutes to eat her bagel and lose herself in someone else's problems.

"They won't stop having sex." Hannah cringed at the overheard comment from the perky brunette she'd met before. Once she'd slept with Mason he'd become like a drug. She just couldn't get her fill of him. "I set out to write romance, but I've ended up with erotica."

"Maybe it's romantica. There are entire e-book sites devoted to the genre." Hannah made a mental note to Google romantica later and shoved a chunk of bagel in her mouth to keep herself from asking for the web address.

"What I have is a hefty pile of sludge and smut. Not publishable. But it got my word count to fifty thousand before midnight. A National Novel Writers Month winner. I finished a novel, and that's what's important."

Hannah smiled and leaned back in the overstuffed chair. She was proud of these ladies for seeing something through to completion. It took dedication not to run scared when things got too tough.

"I want us all to keep in touch, even though the project is over. My address and phone number is in the cards this time. I want to know how everyone fares editing their work." There was a short pause, then a collective gasp from the group. Hannah stuffed her cheeks with the last of her bagel to keep herself from turning around. Enough snooping.

"You're so bad." Hannah recognized the brunette's voice. "I love that about you. Silk stockings by the chimney. Too funny."

"This one is good, but I still like the Santa hat one the best. Or the man wearing it." Hannah's heart stalled in her chest. She knew that card. She tried to chew, to swallow. But her mouth had gone dry, turning the bagel to glue in her mouth.

"I thought the handcuffed Christmas tree was the best. Shackled to the commercialism of the season."

Oh, God. The same cards. Hannah swigged some tea into her mouth to help get the paste down. Even with the bagel stuck in her mouth the tea scalded her tongue.

"I'm glad you liked them," the older woman carrying her dog in a papoose said. "I have one last errand to run. Same time next year?"

Hannah almost choked, but she swallowed the brick and rose from her chair just in time to see the woman walk out the door. She followed, trying to think of just what to do, what to say when she caught up with her. The woman looked about as menacing as a fruit fly.

Hannah halted her pursuit as she watched the woman punch the code and enter the building, her building. Would she drop another card? Hannah wanted to catch her red-handed. Ask her just what she thought she was doing.

Hannah stomped up to the door, punched the code, and marched up the stairs. One flight, two. The woman was fast.

"What do you think you're doing?" Hannah called out as a red envelope fluttered to the ground in front of her door.

"I was just…oh, you're the one."

"Yes, I'm the one who's been getting your anonymous cards." Hannah stepped closer, snatching the envelope.

"You're living with him already? That was quick. Not that I blame you."

"Excuse me?"

"The fireman."

"Firefighter. Firemen are the guys who load coal on trains."

"Really?"

"Yes." Hannah shook her head, finding her indignation again. "What do you mean, we live together? Forget it, I don't want to know. Why have you been leaving those cards?"

"The cards? I pass them out to everyone I know. I got them

for research. I'm a novelist, you see, and my story is about a greeting-card writer and a photographer."

Hannah narrowed her eyes, weighing the woman's animated words. She seemed excited by the situation, as if she had nothing in the world to hide.

"I modeled one of the characters after the fireman, er, firefighter. I recognized him downstairs from the building when he came into the coffee shop. He inspired me. When I saw him downstairs later that day, I watched him check his mail, and—"

"Wait a minute—you live here?" Hannah felt anxious and relieved at the same time. Knowing where the woman lived could help Mason's brother investigate, just to make sure nothing funny was going on.

"Yes, on the first floor. I thought I'd slip a card or two under the door. But now his door seems to be stuck."

"My door. I live here." She stopped short of telling the woman Mason lived upstairs. She looked innocuous, but she was a bit obsessed.

"Oh, how coincidental."

Hannah put her hands on her hips. "My entire family thinks he's terrorizing me!"

The woman arched a bushy eyebrow. "Oh, wonderful! I'll have to work that in during the rewrite."

"Hannah?" That familiar flutter in her stomach started up. How she'd missed that. "What's going on?"

She turned to face him. He was just getting home from work, his duffle in hand. Her mouth watered at the sight. Mason's expression was hopeful behind his tired eyes.

"I got another card." She waved the red envelope in the air. "Actually, they're for you."

His expression fell. "What? Is there a message this time?" Mason glanced past her at the old woman.

"I haven't opened it. I know who's dropping them."

His eyes widened. "You do?"

She figured it out all by herself. No one needed to fix it for her. She smiled and nodded at the woman.

"Hello, I'm Margaret. We met at the coffee shop."

Mason nodded, his brows scrunching. "*You* dropped the cards?" He frowned. "To make it look like I was stalking her?"

Her thin lips twisted in response. "No, of course not! I wanted to make you think you had an admirer, turn the tables a bit. I dropped a card or two on my way back from the write-ins. I was hoping for inspiration. But it looks like I got the apartment wrong." The woman let out a sigh and stroked the head of her dog. "I'm sorry if I caused you any trouble."

"I think you should go." Mason stepped aside on the stairs. The woman nodded and slunked away.

Hannah watched every step, listening intently so she could hear the door open and close at the bottom of the stairs. Should she be worried about Margaret? Was she stalking Mason, or just lonely?

"That's how I felt." Hannah turned to Mason, still standing on the step below her. Eye to eye just like at his parents' house. How did she rewind what had happened and get them back to that moment, before everything had gone wrong? To hell with what people thought, she should have kissed him then as she'd wanted to.

Now, she wasn't going anywhere. And neither was Mason, until she kissed him. Kissing was what they should always be doing, not worrying about besting their siblings' relationship milestones. She licked her lips in anticipation. Peppermint tea like the first time.

Mason's eyes darkened as if he read her mind. He shook his head. "You have to work, and we need to talk first."

She played with the buttons on the front of his shirt and

waited for his eyes to meet hers. She had something she
needed him to know, only she didn't have the words. She
fisted the front of his shirt and pulled him close. She kissed
him hard and deep, letting her tongue massage his into understanding. Her body had known she wanted him from the
first time she'd seen him. Just like this. Her body told her
again when he kissed her. Something in her knew him, always
had and always would. She was learning to listen to her body;
she wondered if he heard it too.

"Hannah." He pulled her from him by the shoulders.
"You're going to be late for work."

"But I just—"

"Just solved your stalker mystery. Congratulations."
Mason picked up his duffle again.

"Your stalker, technically." Hannah reached for him again.
There had to be some way to make him see, to feel what she
felt. How her soul had latched onto his that first time and
would never, ever let go. "Mason, please. I need—"

"I know. And you don't have time right now. It'll keep."

CHAPTER SIXTEEN

"WHY do you drive this old thing?" Hannah asked, climbing in the Bronco. Mason had called and insisted on picking her up from work, and she hadn't fought him. If she took the train she wouldn't make it home before her birthday at midnight.

"Twenty questions already?" he teased, turning the engine over with a roar. "My dad and I rebuilt the engine when I was fifteen. We've been everywhere together. We even took a cross-country trip when Tyler graduated from high school."

Why did men insist on speaking about their vehicles as if they were human? "Doesn't the gas mileage and fuel emissions bother you?"

"Is that your next question? Because according to the rules it is my turn." He pulled out of the parking lot and onto the street. Hannah shook her head and crossed her arms across her chest. "Why don't you have a car?"

She shrugged. "I did, but it died the week before I moved in with Kate. I figured it was a good way to save money. It just isn't efficient to pay to park downtown, especially when we live so close to the train." She turned her body toward his. "My turn. Did your brother check on Margaret?"

"Harmless, I promise. Except that I'll be hearing about it for the next decade from my brothers."

"Are you sure she's not stalking you?"

"Positive. We even talked to some of the people in the writing group. Jeannette e-mailed me her novel, and it's really good." He looked at her. "Really, really good."

"Who's Jeannette?"

"The brunette from the writing group. I'm stalking you in hers, but you fall in love with me anyway. But that's not the best part."

"What's the best part?"

"It's even steamier than your romance novels. Hannah, you're not even trying. I just got you to waste two questions." He shook his head. "It's my turn. How many kids do you want to have?"

Her breath caught. Here we go again. "Mason, let's not go there."

"It's one of those deal breakers you're so worried Kate and Derek haven't figured out yet. Which, by the way, they just want one. Ridiculous in my opinion. Kids need brothers and sisters so there's someone else who knows just how crazy your parents are."

Hannah's head nodded involuntarily. What the hell? "Two or four, definitely an even number. I don't want one of my children to be the fifth wheel like I was. Probably just two; I am turning thirty in about twenty minutes." His warm hand covered hers as he steered their way into the one-way grid of downtown and began to look for a parking place.

She wanted to tell him everything she'd realized in the last few days. How much she loved him, that she'd felt the connection from the second their eyes had met. Would a love-at-first-kiss confession help him forgive her for how impossible she'd been? There had to be some way to show him, more than apologies, more than words.

Hannah let go of his hand and grabbed her bag as he maneuvered next to the curb.

"Where are you going?"

"Home. Or were you planning on sitting in this freezing truck all night?"

"What's in here?" Hannah pulled the square white box from the fridge and set it on the counter. She'd used her key to let them both inside and dropped her bag by the door as if she'd never left.

"One of your birthday presents." He made a show of checking his watch. "You can't open it for two minutes."

"As if." She lifted the lid and peered inside. "Cake. I'm so hungry. I haven't eaten since this morning." She pulled open a drawer and removed two forks, then slammed the drawer shut with her hip. She handed him a fork, but he took them both.

"First you have to make a wish."

Hannah rolled her eyes. "This cake is too small for thirty candles, Mason. If we try it we'll burn the building down and you'll be the laughingstock of your entire department."

Mason undid the sides of the box and slid the cake out. He inserted three long blue candles into the chocolate icing and lit them. "Three wishes. Make them count." He hit the switch turning off the lights.

Hannah tucked the wayward strand of hair not held up by her clip behind her ear. Only the three flickering candles illuminated her face as she bent down. She looked up at him from beneath her lashes. "Who's going to grant my wishes?"

He gripped the counter. "Me."

Her eyes danced in the dim light. "You sure you can give me what I want?"

He swallowed hard. "Absolutely. Anything, anywhere, anytime."

The room went dark, but he could still make out the smoke trails hanging in the air. As he waited for his eyes to adjust he heard the sound of fabric hitting the floor, and two, no, three zippers going down. "I thought you were hungry?" he asked the air in the general direction he thought she was.

His eyes found her, leaning into the open refrigerator, the light inside barely highlighting her heart-shaped bottom teasing him against her pale blue thong.

She straightened back up, the light from inside the fridge silhouetting her hourglass frame in the darkness. "Got it." She turned around, holding up a bottle of champagne. "Will you do the honors?"

He stepped next to her and began untwisting the wires from around the top. Was it possible to uncork champagne in semi-darkness? If not he'd just spray it all over her body and lick it off. He shook his head and concentrated on his task. This was her wish, not his. He saw the carbonation puffing from the top of the bottle as Hannah nudged a wine-glass into his hand. He'd pick up champagne flutes tomorrow. He didn't want to be unprepared again.

He just made out the profile of her neck as she tilted her head back and drained the glass. He heard the glass touch the counter and the clink of forks against the tile.

Chocolate cake was the last thing on his mind. He watched the fork go from the cake to her lips and back to the cake again. Draining his glass, he refilled them both. She moaned as another bite of cake melted in her mouth.

"Where did you get this?" she mumbled as another forkful found its way into her mouth.

She hadn't realized it yet. "You can't guess?"

"I'm not a cake expert." She wet her mouth with the champagne. "Aren't you going to have any?" He reached behind her neck and pulled her close, kissing her deeply. Her voice was breathy as he released her. "I forgot. You like to share chocolate."

She was only eating the ganache from the top, not the filling. Picking up a fork, he slid it through to the center, finding what he was seeking. He lifted the bite to her lips. "Taste."

Her eyes widened at the command but she complied. His eyes didn't leave hers; he didn't want to miss the instant when she realized. She grabbed his wrist. "That's the filling from the truffle. The chili one."

He nodded as she grabbed his face, kissing him again. Short and sweet and happy. "Is the other half peppermint?"

"No, I had to pick one." He'd tried to talk them into it at the chocolate café, but they'd said it wouldn't work. Next year he'd just make it himself.

"So you picked me?" She hopped up on the counter and wiggled her fork around until it was covered with the filling.

"Picked you?" He stepped closer and she widened her legs, allowing him to step inside. He reached behind her and pulled her to the edge of the counter, pressing her heat against him.

"You're the mint." He lifted his champagne from the counter and let her continue. "I'm the chili. We balance each other out. Just like that first night."

He smiled, knowing she'd thought about it. "You're hot, I'll give you that much. But I was not feeling at all balanced that first night." He tipped his glass against her collarbone, watching the liquid trickle down between her breasts. His tongue lapped up every drop. She arched as he neared the edge of each lace cup, but he held off.

She leaned back on her hands, arching her body toward him. He accepted her invitation, pouring the rest of the glass down her body. He traced each trail, over her neck, across the curve of her breast, down her smooth belly to where the champagne dampened the top of her panties.

Straightening up, he found her mouth. She tasted of champagne and chocolate and hot desire. Reaching behind her, he unhooked her bra, letting it fall between them as she shrugged it off. His hands instinctively found her neglected breasts, palming them, flicking the nipples between his fingers until she broke the kiss and arched herself toward him again. He bent his head, tasting them until her skin flushed with heat.

Not yet. "Lift up." She glared at him, but obeyed as he pulled off her underwear. The woman did not like to give up control of anything.

He pulled away and found her champagne glass, trickling it between her parted legs. When she gasped he knelt down, warming her again with his tongue. He'd been trying for a hot and cold contrast, but the bubbles were amazing. He pulled back and tried it again; this time she pulled him forward by his hair. With a powerful scream she came hard, releasing him and pounding her fists against the tile of the counter before her body relaxed into a heap. Gathering her in his arms, he carried her to the bedroom, laying her across the bed as he kissed his way up her body.

His mouth centered on that spot between her ear and jaw that always made her dig her toes into the bed. "Mason, please," she moaned before crushing her mouth against his. Her fingers threaded through his hair, pulling him closer, and closer.

Peeling her fingers away, he dove for the nightstand. Why hadn't he thought to have condoms on the bed already? His hand dug through the drawer in the dark, encountering everything but what he sought. Finally he grabbed the box and pulled it out.

Empty. No way. He sat up on the bed and looked through

the drawer. Nothing. Mason tried to will blood into his brain. There must be some condoms in this apartment somewhere. Wallet. He put one in there. If not there was a box in her nightstand downstairs.

He leaned back down on the bed and she grabbed his head and pulled him in for another bruising kiss.

"Hannah, I'll be right back," he whispered against her cheek.

"No," she growled, pulling him down on top of her and wrapping a leg around his thigh. He pushed down on the bed. If she kept this up much longer there would be no need for a condom any more.

"Birth control," he ground out through his clenched jaw.

"You said anything." The other leg wrapped around him and she shifted beneath him. The feel of her slick heat against him took his breath away. "I don't want anything between us."

"You're sure?" he asked, barely able to contain himself. He'd never had sex without a condom. Never realized how much he wanted to until now. A secret thrill rolled through him as she ground her body against his. He felt her, every nuance of the exquisite fire that burned in her soul.

Her fingers wrapped around his shoulders and she arched against him in response. Did she realize what could happen?

"Hannah, honey, even if I pull out, you could get pregnant."

"You said anything." She kissed him with such a fever he almost lost himself. Kissed him until he knew she was as sure as he had always been.

"Will you look at me?" He wanted to watch her, to see that she felt it too. Her eyes fluttered open. Dark and glassy and though he couldn't make out the color in the dim light he knew they were green.

He met her gaze as he entered her slowly, carefully, wanting to remember how every inch felt. He watched her eyes close and he stilled himself. Something was glistening from the corner of her eye. Swiping his thumb across her eyelid, he brushed away the tear and she bit her lip. Her legs wrapped tighter, pressing against him. He reached down and held her hips still. "Did I hurt you?"

She shook her head, but her eyes stayed shut.

The sensation of filling her with nothing between them was exquisite. So much more than he had anticipated. "Look at me."

Her head moved from side to side again. He watched as her mouth opened and twisted before she pressed her lips together again.

"Hannah, I love you." He felt as overwhelmed as she did, but he had to make sure that was all it was. "Please just look at me."

Tears leaked from the sides as she opened them, a sob racking her body as she pulled him down into a kiss that sucked the breath from his lungs. He reached for her hands, linking his fingers with hers as he began to move deep within her. Long and strong and steady. He wanted this to last, for her to feel how long they would last. He wanted to erase the last vestiges of doubt from her mind by erasing them from her body.

Too soon her breath was catching, her temperature rising. The waves of her release built around him, his own body responding to hers. In some inexplicable way her climax pulled him deeper and deeper into her body, so deep he actually felt the pleasure of her release as she went over the edge. His jaw clenched as he forced himself to stay aware as he followed her over.

Their bodies were still slick with sweat, their breathing still ragged and uneven when he awoke. He couldn't have been out long. He should release his hold on her, let her go and tuck her in bed. But the thought of it was painful. He reached around, pulling the comforter over the top of them as he snuggled her closer. "I love you, Hannah," he whispered as he drifted off.

"You'd better," she murmured against his chest.

"Is that mine or yours?" Hannah asked without opening her eyes. It had to be too early for a phone call, though with the drapes in Mason's bedroom she never knew what time it was.

"It's yours." He pulled her closer, as if it weren't the third time the phone had rung this morning.

"I got one for you." It was her birthday; she didn't have to answer the phone if she didn't want to.

"One what?" He yawned and nestled further into the bed. She loved how he could just fall back asleep. Some day she'd have to learn how to do that.

"A cell phone. It's downstairs. I ordered it when I got my promotion and couldn't get hold of you." She twisted her finger in his chest hair, focusing on a single strand. "It came while you weren't talking to me." She yanked the hair out.

Mason yelped and clasped his hand over hers. "I was waiting for you to tell me what you wanted."

She'd walked right into that open manhole. "I still have a wish left. I wish to never talk about that again. Ever."

"Very mature for someone who is supposed to be a year older." Mason's landline rang on the nightstand behind them. "What time is it anyway?" Hannah watched his muscles ripple as he pulled himself to sitting beside her. She laid her head back on the pillow and watched him answer the phone.

"Hello? Goodbye, Derek. What? Okay." He hung up the phone and looked at her. "You need to answer your phone.

It's your sister, something about coming over. She had Troy call Derek to call here. Sisters are weird, aren't they?"

"That doesn't make any sense." Hannah sat up just as her phone chirped to life. Jumping from the bed, she grabbed a T-shirt from the closet and found her phone in her bag just as she pulled the shirt over her head.

"Guess what, Hannah?" Molly's voice sounded much too chipper for morning. Hannah glanced at the clock on the VCR. It was noon. "Mom and I are circling the block, looking for a parking space. Mom wanted to surprise you with a day at the spa. You must have been in the shower, otherwise you would have answered your phone."

"No," Hannah snapped into the receiver.

"Yes. I see it, Mom, but I'm sure we can get a closer spot."

"I have to shower."

"Of course, finish your shower. I'll let us in with my key."

"Thank you, thank you, thank you." Hannah slammed the phone shut and grabbed her bag. She'd get the rest of it later. Except she'd need pants to go downstairs. Where had she taken off her pants?

"What was that about?" Mason asked from the bedroom doorway, still gloriously naked. Damned tease.

"My mom and sister are about to knock on my door."

Mason shrugged. "Tell them to come up here."

Finally! She found her pants and tried to put them on so fast she fell against the refrigerator. "I can't do that, Mason. My mother would have a heart attack if I even suggested it."

"You're an adult. I'm sure she can take the shock." He thought she was kidding.

"My parents don't believe in sex outside of marriage." He was going to laugh. "I'm serious here. That's why we can't live together."

Shoes weren't necessary, wherever they were. She was

halfway out the door, but turned before she closed it. "We are having a family birthday dinner at a restaurant my mom heard about, Mon Desir, at six-thirty. Can you come?"

He nodded, a smirk still playing on his lips.

"Better yet, come at seven and I'll pretend to be sick so we can leave. I probably won't have to pretend around all that French food."

"Why are you going to a French restaurant? It's your birthday."

Hannah shrugged. "My mom loves French food and I figure she did all the work to give me a birthday in the first place. After, we'll go out for fried chicken. You'll come?"

"I wouldn't miss it."

CHAPTER SEVENTEEN

"I CAN'T believe Mom just bailed like that." Hannah wiggled her painted pink toes as Molly drove to the restaurant.

Molly shrugged as she took the tunnel away from downtown. "She said it was a nasty headache. I'm just glad Dad could come get her so we could stay. I loved my massage."

"Me, too; I nearly fell asleep." Admiring the pale pink polish on her fingernails, Hannah looked at the scenery. "Where exactly is this restaurant?"

"Don't worry. Troy always makes sure I have directions before he lets me go anywhere these days. The first few months it was cute, but it's already getting old."

Hannah opened her mouth to ask a million questions that were none of her business, and closed it again. It was her birthday, and she didn't want to fight with Molly. "Thanks again for the save this morning. Mom's head might have exploded if she caught me coming down the stairs."

"Consider it your birthday present. You sure didn't make it easy on me. You could have answered your phone."

Getting out of bed would have meant the night was over and she was still mourning the loss of it. It had been perfect. The perfect way to show him how completely she loved him. "Next time I will."

Molly exited the freeway. "I still can't believe you were the one to solve the mystery of the cards. I'm sorry I didn't believe you when you said they weren't from Mason. I know Troy was hard on you both."

She didn't know the half of it. "Are you sure your directions are right? This looks awfully residential." Not that she would mind being late for dinner. Her mother always ordered the most disgusting appetizers.

Molly's grip on the steering wheel tightened. "I know where I'm going. Is Mason going to be there?"

"Yes, but he'll be late. He had something he couldn't get out of." And something he needed to help her get out of.

"That doesn't bother you? I know you hate it when people are late."

Hannah waved her hand through the air. "He's never late, and when he might be he always lets me know ahead of time."

"So what is wrong with him? You can usually reduce a man to his faults in five minutes or less."

"There is nothing wrong with him." The edge in her voice surprised her.

Flipping open her cell phone, Molly hit a speed-dial button. "You really like him, don't you?"

"Mason? Of course I like him." Hannah arched an eyebrow as Molly flipped the phone closed again and shoved it back in her purse without saying a word. "What are you doing?"

"Just checking to see if Troy would answer." Molly turned into a neighborhood Hannah vaguely recognized. "Do you love him?"

What was it with people and that question? "I don't see how that's any of your business." She hadn't managed to go there with Mason yet; no way was she previewing her revelation to her sister. She loved him, and he was overdue to find out. "Where are we going?"

"We're here," Molly said, pulling into a driveway behind Mason's Bronco.

Hannah looked around them. His parents' house. There were cars everywhere, even Kate's. *What the hell?*

Hannah jumped as her car door opened. Mason. Swinging her legs out, she looked up at him. "What's going on?"

He took her hand and pulled her to her feet. "Dinner. You hate French food."

"You tricked me!" She grinned and stepped closer, suddenly remembering she hadn't kissed him goodbye this morning.

"We surprised you." He stepped away, pulling her toward the house. "Come on, your mom even made the fried chicken."

Hannah froze. The last time she'd asked her mother to make fried chicken, she had been sixteen. Her mother had tried some low-fat oven-fried boneless chicken breast concoction that had tasted like leather rolled in sawdust.

Taking both her hands, Mason dragged her to the house. "Don't worry. I supervised."

Mason couldn't believe he'd ever considered doing this before last night. Even now that he was sure of her answer he was sweating. There was no way he'd make it through dinner; he wasn't going to be able to eat a thing.

He had to stick to the plan. It was a good plan, well thought out, and she'd love it. But watching her make nice with Kate and his mother across the room made him want to tug her into a closet and just beg. Get it over with.

Kate had planned to fly in as a surprise all along. She hadn't missed Hannah's birthday in ten years. Mason was glad she'd had a chance to check the ring. And then so had her mother, and his, and Tara, and even Riana. They all thought it was perfect, but he wondered if she would have preferred to pick it out herself. She was such a paradigm of modern independence and old-fashioned tradition he never knew which way she'd go. And he hoped he never would.

After a quick peek in the kitchen Mason made his way to Hannah. "Dinner's almost ready," he said, refilling her champagne glass.

"With all this champagne you would think we're celebrating something." She looked at him pointedly. Mason stared hard at Kate. She'd better not have said anything.

Kate raised her glass. "To never having to relive your twenties."

The rest of the family joined in the toast as Mason breathed a sigh of relief. He was wound so tight he might snap. His mother and Kate excused themselves to help serve and Tara chased Riana through the house, leaving them as close to alone as they had been since he'd ushered her through the front door.

Hannah turned on him. "I don't know whether to kiss you or kick you. How could you arrange for our families to meet without telling me?"

Mason stepped back, just in case. "Given the choice, always kiss me." The look on her face told him that was not going to happen any time soon. "I thought it would be a nice birthday surprise. It gets you out of eating foie gras, doesn't it?"

Hannah shuddered. "True. But this could have gone very badly."

Forever the optimist. "But it didn't. They had to meet some time. And they get along great. Our moms have been cooking up a storm all afternoon, and my dad hasn't been to the garage once."

Swirling what was left of her champagne, Hannah looked up at him. "Exactly when did you plan this?"

Mason shrugged. *Careful*. "A few days ago, but we changed the menu this morning when you mentioned fried chicken. Until then we were doing meat loaf."

"You planned this after you broke up with me." Hannah finished the last of her champagne, eyeing him over the rim of the glass.

"I set it up while you were deciding what you wanted."

"Even after all the nasty things we said, you still knew."

Mason nodded, trading his full glass for her empty one.

"Careful, or I might think you are trying to get me drunk." Her lips kissed the edge of the glass as she looked up at him.

"I've never had you drunk, but I bet it will be fantastic." She lowered the glass as he leaned in.

"Everything's ready," Mary Jean sang from the kitchen.

Mason groaned and took Hannah's hand as they made their way to the dining room. He was stuck all the way across the table from her. Her parents sat on either side of her, monopolizing her attention when she wasn't devouring the meal of fried chicken, chipotle macaroni and cheese, maple-glazed carrots, and green beans with butter and almonds.

Mason could barely stand to eat until she locked his ankle between hers beneath the table. It was strange how such a simple act relaxed and reassured him. Amazing how she communicated more clearly with her body than with her words.

After dinner the crowd dispersed into the living room. "Time for presents!" Derek carried the boxes out from the closet where they'd been hidden.

Hannah's face lit up as she sat on the couch. "This is the best birthday I've had since I was a kid. Food and friends and family and presents too. And I was worried about turning thirty."

While everyone was laughing Mason handed Hannah his gift. "Mine first." She took the lid off the tiny black box and pulled out the small velvet box inside. She shot him such a scathing look that it made him wonder about his plans for the rest of his life. "Just open it."

The box creaked open and she gasped. Her eyes danced before her mouth fell into a grin. "They don't match."

She held up the single emerald and single sapphire earrings for the family to see. The stones were genuine and hazy, like her eyes.

"They match you."

"Thank you, I love them." She kissed his hand before going on to the rest of her gifts. Not quite the thank you he'd been hoping for, but the best he could expect with both her and his parents in the room.

"This is officially the best birthday ever." Her face shone as she tucked away a set of red velour pajamas from her mother. Velour had potential. Completely covered and utterly touchable. Kate and Molly's gift hadn't made it out of the bag, but it was great if her blush was any indication. His folks gave her champagne flutes. Odd, because he hadn't mentioned they needed them.

Mason swallowed hard and wished his stomach weren't flopping around like a fish out of water. "There's one more." He stood and reached for the box that had been burning a hole in his pocket for a week. He took a deep breath, two, and knelt next to her. Her eyes glazed over as he took her hand and began to speak.

"I have loved you from the first minute I saw you. I was drawn to you in a way I hope I never understand. One minute I was alone and the next I was madly in love with you. And I didn't need to know your name. I just needed for you to let me love you." This box opened silently. No one in the room was breathing. "Marry me."

Her eyes focused on the ring, his face, and then the ring

again. Maybe he should have just shown her the solitaire. But Kate had insisted he have the band that held the emerald and sapphire that matched her earrings flanking the ring. Her breath quickened as she looked at him again.

"Mason, I..." Her eyes skipped over him and zeroed in on her father. "Daddy, I didn't know."

The older man chuckled. "I did, honey, and you have our blessing."

Her eyes closed as she gripped his hand. "You asked my father?"

"I knew you'd want me to." She pulled her hand away and covered her mouth as tears squeezed from her eyes.

"It's just a lot to take in. I wasn't expecting...and everyone is here." She took a long breath to steady herself. Grasping his hand in hers, she looked him in the eye. "Why now?"

She had to ask after last night? "Until now I wasn't sure you'd say yes." Hannah stole a glance at Kate and Derek. Mason shook his head. "We're not in competition with anyone. I'll wait until you're ready."

"You'll wait?"

As if he had a choice. "Anytime, anywhere."

She leaned forward and pressed her forehead against his. He closed his eyes as their breathing synchronized and slowed. *Just say yes.*

"January."

His eyes flew open. What did that mean? "January what?"

Glassy, almost green eyes stared at him. "Eighth. Before we go to New Zealand."

His heart skipped in his chest. "Is that a yes?"

Before she nodded a second time he kissed her, swallowing her laughter as he went.

"Hands where I can see them, Mason," Mac's voice said from somewhere far away. "You're not married yet."

MILLS & BOON®

0506/01b

Live the emotion

Modern
romance™

HIS PRIVATE MISTRESS by Chantelle Shaw

Rafael Santini and Eden Lawrence's passionate relationship ended in betrayal and deceit. Only now Rafael is determined to make her his mistress once more. Eden may be older and wiser, but she is still unable to resist the only man she has ever loved…

BERTOLUZZI'S HEIRESS BRIDE by Catherine Spencer

Falling in love is not on Natalie Cavanaugh's agenda – particularly not with notorious Demetrio Bertoluzzi… Natalie finds herself drawn to him like a moth to the flame. But to surrender her innocence to this allegedly dangerous man could be her undoing…

CAPTIVE IN HIS BED by Sandra Marton

When Matthew Knight accepts the case of missing Mia Palmieri, the only way to unearth the truth is to kidnap her! But, while Mia is held prisoner in Matthew's luxury hideaway, she can't resist his hard muscled handsomeness…

KEPT BY THE TYCOON by Lee Wilkinson

Madeleine Knight gave Rafe Lombard her heart, but when she learnt secrets of his past she knew he would never be hers – so she ran. Rafe is determined to prove that no woman leaves him without his say-so and wants Madeleine back by his side…

On sale 2nd June 2006

Available at WHSmith, Tesco, ASDA, Borders, Eason, Sainsbury's and most bookshops

www.millsandboon.co.uk